HELEN DUNMORE

Love of Fat Men

VIKING

VIKING

Published by the Penguin Group
Penguin Books Ltd, 27 Wrights Lane, London w8 5tz, England
Penguin Books USA Inc., 375 Hudson Street, New York, New York 10014, USA
Penguin Books Australia Ltd, Ringwood, Victoria, Australia
Penguin Books Canada Ltd, 10 Alcorn Avenue, Toronto, Ontario, Canada m4v 3b2
Penguin Books (NZ) Ltd, 182–190 Wairau Road, Auckland 10, New Zealand

Penguin Books Ltd, Registered Offices: Harmondsworth, Middlesex, England

This selection first published 1997
1 3 5 7 9 10 8 6 4 2

Copyright © Helen Dunmore 1990, 1992, 1993, 1994, 1995, 1997
The moral right of the author has been asserted
The Acknowledgements on p. vii constitute an extension of this copyright page

Set in 11½/14½pt Monophoto Garamond
Filmset by Datix International Limited, Bungay, Suffolk
Printed in England by Clays Ltd, St Ives plc

A CIP catalogue record for this book is available from the British Library

ISBN 0-670-86293-2

List of Contents

Acknowledgements

Love of Fat Men was first published in *Stand* 33/1, 1991

Batteries was first published in . . . *And a Happy New Year*, ed. Campbell, Hallett, Palmer and Woolsey, Women's Press, 1993

Short Days, Long Nights was first published in *London Magazine*, vol. 29, 11 & 12, 1990, and subsequently in *Best Short Stories of 1992*, ed. Giles Gordon, Heinemann

Spring Wedding was first published in *New Writing* 4, ed. A. S. Byatt and Alan Hollinghurst, Vintage, 1995

Annina was first published in *Caught in a Story*, ed. Caroline Heaton and Christine Park, Vintage, 1992

The Ice Bear was first published in *A Bridport Harvest*, 1990

The Orang-utans and the Angry Woman was first published in *Iron Women*, ed. Kitty Fitzgerald, Iron Press, 1990

Ullikins was first published in *Irish Tatler*, December 1994

A Grand Day was broadcast on BBC Radio 4 in July 1994

Smell of Horses and *Girls on Ice* were first published in *Writing Women*, 8/2 & 3, and 10/2

Love of Fat Men

LOVE OF FAT MEN. Ulli would like to go and see a film with this title. She would buy herself a fistful of Panda liquorice and a daytime ticket and sit there and watch it through again and again, until the usherette sent for the manager. And another good thing about films is that people who are of average weight in real life look dense, almost majestic, once they are on film. Because the camera loves absences. Flesh that isn't there. Hollows under cheekbones. A shadow under the jaw which writes a whole false story of intellect and suffering into the face of a man who spends all day wondering whether he has done right to have both ears pierced, or should he have left it at one?

Speaking of earrings, she loves them too. She thinks of a man who was in a promising way to be fat one day. For now he makes do with a curve of the jowl, a faint trace that time will roll out in flesh. Around his lips there is a gloss of oil. He has always just finished eating spaghetti. And not cheap dried macaroni either. He has a pasta machine in his kitchen. He strips off long ribbons of slippery translucent dough and coats them in virgin green olive oil and eats them just as they are. He says it is a waste of time trying to make sauce with the tomatoes they grow in this country, which are only fit for throwing at politicians. Instead of this he makes anchovy spaghetti and tagliatelle with pesto for his friends, which they eat with strong sharp wine. An hour or two later they are

1

hungry again. His name is Lucca, like the city. Or at least, this is what he calls himself. He has a family which is even more secret than her own. But she hopes that she will not discover one day that Lucca has a mother and father sitting in a one-bedroom apartment in the outskirts of Helsinki, dreaming of their summer house, and visits from Lucca. She likes small lies to remain as they are, seductive, growing their own flesh out of hints and silences. What a tombstone it would make, too. Here lies a liar.

Ulli knows she isn't Lucca's type. But he is fond of her. He is her friend. Ulli's not being his type means that he can come round to her room and sprawl on her bed eating packets of macaroons or Danish pastries which he has bought at a cake shop in the city centre. He makes quite a long detour in order to buy these particular macaroons, fragile and yet chewy at the centre, flavoured with almonds rather than with almond essence. When Lucca has been spending the afternoon in Ulli's room, there are crackling crumbs in the bed all night and transparent grease stains on the quilt cover. But she doesn't mind. He buys tiny triangular apricot pastries for her, and makes better coffee to go with them than she ever makes herself. Come to think of it that is the only time he stands up. When Lucca visits, he lies.

He asks Ulli about what he refers to as her love-life. In the hope that it will stop him using this expression, which she dislikes, Ulli has told him that her own grandmother used to ask exactly the same question, when Ulli was about sixteen.

'How's your love-life, Ulli?'

Ulli pictures her love-life as an elusive but rapacious animal which nobody else has ever seen. This is why they keep asking after it.

Lucca always smells so clean. He smells of clean cotton

and sharp lemon soap and almonds and vanilla. Sometimes he smells of sugar, but she doesn't like that so much. Or he smells of garlic and wine, and the parsley he chews after meals to freshen his breath. Lucca is the only person she has ever seen eating a bunch of parsley sprig by sprig. It is full of iron, he tells her. If she eats enough garlic and parsley she will get through the whole winter without flu or a cold.

Ulli is not Lucca's type, but he likes her hair, because it is long and very soft, with a watery feel to it when it is newly washed. He feels that he could look after it better than she does herself. So sometimes she'll give it over to him for the afternoon. Her head goes with it of course, but they don't mind that. She sits on the floor by the bed and Lucca rolls over so that he can spread the hair out over the quilt, lift it and brush it out and run his hands down it, then plait it again. He can do a French plait, and once he has done this Ulli wriggles away from him, because she likes this style and is not able to do it for herself. But as soon as he has done it he always wants to unplait it again, to stroke and weigh and twist the hair into new shapes, to let it drop free. Sometimes he plaits ribbons into it. Sometimes he puts it up and pins it on the top of her head. But it's too severe for her like that, he says. It will suit her better when she's older. He tells her how she will look when she is thirty, if she is lucky and things go well for her. He says that she's lazy and she ought to have her hair trimmed regularly at the hairdresser's, instead of letting one of her girlfriends snip round the bottom of it with a pair of cheap sewing scissors.

'It saves money,' says Ulli. 'You aren't going to eat all that macaroon, are you? Let me have the outside bits.'

She is not Lucca's type, but he says that she reminds him of his sisters. He doesn't say much about them, but she has the impression that they are a little younger than she is, still at home, three girls with long hair and lively sliding eyes, crammed into one bedroom with pictures of Switzerland on the wall. No pop stars. They like Switzerland, for some reason. The eldest of them is planning to work there as an au pair, before she goes to college. They are all bright girls, Lucca says, much brighter than he is. He says they adore speaking English.

Lucca's sisters do not live in jeans like Ulli. They make their own clothes: suits and skirts and fitted jackets. Then they lend them to one another, because they are all as near the same size as makes no difference, and they go out on summer evenings in jade-green, in cerise, in butter-yellow, in soft cream. Ulli wonders if they are still virgins. Perhaps they would have to be, in one room. Or perhaps there is a system for sharing the men, as there is for sharing the clothes, so that no one gets over-attached to one garment, or one manner of making love.

Next week, Lucca says, he has been asked to a party in the country about fifty kilometres away. Does Ulli want to come?

'Will your sisters be there?' asks Ulli.

'Of course not! What would my sisters be doing at such a party? They wouldn't know anybody.'

'Will I?'

'Oh, I should think so. One or two. And anyway you'll like the others. They'll be your type.'

'How do we get there? I'm not going on the bus.'

'I've fixed it. We're borrowing a car.'

'Whose?'

'I don't think you know him.'

'Come round on the Friday then, and put my hair in a French plait.'

'Not if you're going to wear those jeans.'

'Fine, I'll wear it loose.'

She stands up and nearly treads on their dirty coffee cups. Lucca smiles at her from the bed. Looking at him from this angle, she thinks that it is a pity she is not his type.

By midnight on Saturday Ulli knows that she's not going to meet anyone at the party. Only half an hour ago the rooms were thick with dancers. People were spilling out on to the wooden veranda and into the garden beyond to enjoy the mothy dusk of a summer night. Couples drifted under the trees, twining and consuming one another. If you blinked, they were gone.

And they've gone. Strangers, acquaintances, lovers, it's all one now. It doesn't matter. For those who've found some-body, all that matters is now. For those who've found some-body the night has narrowed to an intake of breath, and a little pulse of sweat. They laugh with eagerness. They sprawl and ache on the sand down by the shore. They share a ciga-rette and blur each other's lips with dry whispers. Ulli steps out on to the veranda and sips from her potent little glass of mesimarja. The dew settles on her bare arms. The rail of the veranda is damp. Its paint peels under her hands. The family is not staying here this summer. There will be a party or two, a weekend, perhaps some sailing. But nobody will have time to sand down the veranda railings and coat them with primer and paint them so that they last through the winter ahead. That's the kind of job you do when you go to the summer house for weeks on end, the kind of job you do towards the middle of August when the days are already getting shorter and you are starting to think of berry picking and mushroom gathering in the forest. And hauling the boat out of the water to clean the hull. Ulli has never been to this summer house before, but it's familiar to her as her own breath.

The air smells of raspberries, but it's still too dark for her to see where they are growing. She takes another sip of her drink. She's hardly drunk anything tonight, just a couple of glasses of white wine with blackcurrant syrup in them, and now this. She has eaten some birthday cake, a cake with TIMMO on it in dull silver pearls.

Someone whistles. She starts and looks round. A dark shape detaches itself from the door. It's Lucca. He comes over to her and stands very close, so close that she can smell his white cottony smell, and again the smell of raspberries.

'We're going fishing,' he says. 'Do you want to come?'

'Who's we?'

'Just me and Timmo. You remember, I introduced you to Timmo. It's his house.'

'Why don't they come here any more?'

Lucca shrugs.

'The kids are grown up. And his mother's got something wrong with her. Multiple sclerosis. She can't get about.'

'Do you know her?'

'Oh yes.'

'It seems sad to leave it like this. The house.'

'Timmo comes here sometimes.'

'With you?'

'Sometimes.'

They walk down the path through the woods, to the little jetty. It is closer to one than twelve now, and the midsummer dawn's breaking. Timmo is sitting at the end of the jetty. He has cast his line already. The water is so still that Ulli can see his float, scarcely moving.

Ulli sits on the silvery wood, tucking her heels under her. A breeze draws across the surface of the lake, wrinkling it. It reminds Ulli of her mother making jam. She would drop a spoonful on to a clean saucer and blow on it. If it wrinkled, it was ready to pot. Lucca and Timmo speak very softly so as not to frighten the fish. This is the best time for fishing, Timmo says. They sit for a long time, fishing and catching nothing. Ulli is glad. She does not want to see the jetty bloodied with slippery, mauled fish. Lucca has a bar of dark bitter chocolate, which he breaks carefully in three pieces. They eat it, and Ulli throws tiny crumbs into the reedy water under the jetty.

'Come and sit here,' Lucca says to her. 'You can't see anything back there.' He shifts sideways and makes room for her.

'Quite a party, wasn't it?' says Timmo.

'It was fine,' says Ulli, 'but a bit too couply for me.'

'I know what you mean,' says Timmo. 'Well, this fishing is a dead loss. Never mind.'

Ulli's feet are getting cold. She shivers and rubs them together.

'Parties, parties,' says Lucca. 'Turn round, Ulli, and you can put your feet under Timmo's coat while I plait your hair.'

Timmo sighs and leans back, gripping the rod between his knees. He spreads out a fold of his coat and wraps it around Ulli's feet. It's one of those family coats that doesn't really belong to anyone, and is kept on a peg by the back door for people to grab as they go out of the house to fish or to chop wood in the chill of early morning. It must have been an expensive coat once, but now it's scored with thorns and berry stains, and the lining's torn. It smells of moss. A few hundred metres downshore, where a bathing-hut's rimmed by the sunrise, Ulli sees a flicker of movement. A figure steps out on to a frail-looking jetty, like their own. It bends, unpacking fishing equipment.

'A serious fisherman, that one,' says Timmo. 'He's down here every morning.'

It's two thirty. The sun's fully up now, hazily wrapped in blue. It's going to be hot again. Why sleep, why go back to the house, why waste a single hour of the summer's day that's just joined on flawlessly to the one before, thinks Ulli, as her feet begin to tingle with the warmth from under Timmo's coat. She smells moss and chocolate and the sharp mineral smell of lake water. Why not stay all day? Later they'll bathe, the three of them. She'll find little wild raspberries, so ripe they are almost purple, the sort that dissolve in your mouth leaving only a grainy rub of seed against your teeth. She shuts her eyes.

'Lucca,' she says. She's going to tell him about the day ahead. There's no need to go home. They can stay here, just the three of them . . .

'What?' asks Lucca, finishing off the plait. Each woven strand of hair is cold and perfect as the scale of a fish.

But Ulli doesn't answer. She's already asleep.

Batteries

She looks him dead in the eye.

'There – are – no – more – batteries,' she repeats.

His face wrinkles. 'But you said! You said you'd bought batteries and all. You told us we had to write down everything we wanted on our lists and I did, I made a list and it had batteries on it because I knew I'd need them if I got a Gameboy and –'

'I did buy batteries,' she cuts in. 'They're all used up. You used them all. None of us knew how quick that Gameboy would go through batteries. You can plug it into the mains, can't you?'

He stands in front of her, crumpled and reddening. It is 2 p.m. and they have had the stockings, the presents under the tree, drinks before dinner, the dinner. When he crashed into the kitchen for his batteries Paula was putting away the blue and white pudding dishes she'd brought to the cottage all the way from the city so they could have their exotic fruit salad off the china they always used at Christmas. Lychees, passion-fruit, kumquats, starfruit, tangerines with waxy leaves on their stems, glowing slices of mango lapping pineapple on the white platter her mother had left her. She brought the fruit from the city, too, padded in tissue and wrapped in brown paper bags so it wouldn't ripen too fast. Let other families gorge on heavy puddings.

'It's a Gameboy,' Kay whinges. 'My Sega plugs into the

9

mains. I don't want to plug my *Gameboy* –'

Eric must have caught what Kay was saying. Paula heard his feet quick-padding overhead, up to the bedroom. Now he comes back and stands dramatically in the kitchen doorway, hands behind his back. He smiles.

'Here's Father Christmas,' he says.

The boy's face changes. It's all going to start again. Presents and paper and tearing and finding and having and batteries and – *'That's it now kids, you've had all your presents for this year,'* Paula said at midday, when he and Maudie finished scouring under the tree. But she was wrong. Kay shoots her a look and then begins to clamour round his father.

'Dad, what is it, what've you got, Dad –'

'Hey, hey, steady now. Thought I heard someone asking about batteries,' and, over his son's head, to his wife, 'I guessed this would happen. Those things eat up juice.' He brings his hands from behind his back and there it is, a white box with a transparent top and four fat cylinders nestled in it.

'Wow, Dad! A battery charger. Wow, c'n I –'

'Yeah. Now careful, son, it's all fixed up. I been charging these batteries since last night.'

Paula watches their two heads duck over the plastic box. Her boy is shining now.

'Now mind,' warns the father, 'it's for Maudie too.'

'Maudie hasn't even got a Gameboy.'

'She has her Walkman,' says Paula.

'That uses different batteries,' slaps back Kay.

'Where is Maudie?' asks Eric, and they look round, and listen. Paula goes to the living-room and there is Maudie, curled in a chair, thumb jammed in her mouth, staring not at the video which is running through for the second time but at the white space of the window. She's OK. Paula returns to the kitchen. The Gameboy winks, back in command.

'Will you take that thing out of here,' she says.

'You gave it to me,' mutters Kay.

'Come on, son, come on upstairs and I'll give you a game. Your mother's tired.'

Paula kicks a tired piece of wrapping paper under the table. Batteries. She lets her arms flop on the table, and her head go down. The children hate to see her like this. Two seventeen on Christmas afternoon.

If it was a proper winter they'd be outdoors, skiing. Pack the children into their snowsuits until they're as fat as bears. Get the four pairs of skis from the shed and go out into the cold blue afternoon, over Silverhill and down to the flats where it was easy skiing for the kids. But there's no skiing this year. Night after night the ground freezes. It is black and hard a foot deep. Bushes lean skinnily against the wind, dying. They will die without the comfort of snow. On TV they show birds dropping through the pall of frost, dead on the wing. One day parents were warned to keep home their children under ten. Even in the city Paula kept Kay and Maudie home, warmed by the steady breath of central heating, while dossers collapsed in the iron-hard park. Paula's breath froze on her lips. Her nose ran and the snot made curls of frost. But there was no snow. The sky was hard and cloudless by day. By night it was jabbed by icy stars and a thin wind turned overcoats to cotton. The climate's changing, people said, as they looked for the snow.

Paula stares out of the kitchen window. There is no wind now, only a quiet shudder of cold in the pine branches. It is grey, a close, tight-knit grey. Is it warmer? Will the sky yellow and thicken and send down the snow? She goes to the window and squints at the outdoor thermometer. It is a couple of degrees warmer. If the temperature went up a few more degrees they might have snow. She hears Kay babbling to Maudie in the living-room. He is telling her how Mom forgot to buy enough batteries, but it was OK because Dad bought a battery charger. Amazing. Brilliant. Brilliant Dad.

Paula steps quietly to the hallway. She fetches out her ski-trousers as Kay clatters past her, back upstairs to Dad and the Gameboy. He does not stop to ask what she's doing. Paula puts on ski-trousers and jacket, gloves, cap with ear-flaps. She kneels down and reaches into the rack at the side of the cupboard, and takes out her skates. Just then Maudie stumbles through the door, her eyes glazed with sleep.

'Mom,' she pipes, 'where're you going?'

'Ssh. Nowhere.'

'Why're you putting on all your stuff?'

'Maudie, go on back to the living-room. D'you want another video?'

Paula keeps the videos hidden. The children are not allowed more than one each day. Maudie's face brightens, she nearly fastens on the bribe, then,

'Can I come with you? Please?'

'No, Maudie. It's too cold.'

'I've got my new snowsuit.' Maudie is already pulling off her slippers. 'Please, Mom, please.'

'No,' says Paula, and she picks up her skates. She opens the door to a slice of freezing air and turns her back on Maudie.

'Go on back in the house. Now.'

The track rings under her boots. Frost seized the ground suddenly, weeks back, leaving steely ripples of mud. Over there, behind the fir trees, is the slim, frozen tongue of the lake. It is shallow here, spread out into fingers on which the cottages sit. Paula walks fast to the shore.

She sits on a rock and fits on her skates. They have skated most days and the bay is full of blade marks. But they have not gone far. And Kay has been stupid, throwing stones on to the ice. She slapped him for it.

'What if someone broke a leg because of you?'

Usually they take their broom down to the lake and sweep a small rink for themselves, but this year there is no need. There is no snow on the ice. Paula knows where it is safe to skate. She has been coming here all her life, and even if she hadn't she would be safe this year. There has never been a frost like it. The whole lake is solid, even by the springs. There are not many people here for Christmas this year, because there is no snow.

Today the lake is bare. She looks south and sees where it widens, the ice pale and empty, waiting for her. She stands up, staggering a little on her skates, as the wine she drank at dinner sings in her head. It is so cold. Her face is covered but for a strip of flesh around her eyes. She is ready. She bends forward, puts her weight on her right blade, pushes off. The ice is perfect. In a few strokes she shoots out beyond the churned ice. She will do some figures first. She never has time when the kids are there, pestering her to watch them, to admire them. Eric doesn't like to skate, never has done. She does a T-stop, turns to shore, prepares to skate backwards and then come round in a tight circle, just there – and there's Maudie, running down the bank, her red cap flapping, her skates in her hand.

'Mom! Mom!' she screams. 'Wait for me!'

Paula stands frozen. There is Maudie in royal blue on the shore, waving frantically. There behind her is the sweep of fir which hides the cottage where Eric and Kay crouch over the Gameboy, and the spare set of batteries recharges in the battery charger Eric has been thoughtful enough to buy and bring all the way up here without telling Paula. Three hisses escape through the fine wool scarf which hides Paula's lips.

'Batteries. Jesus. Christmas.'

Something wicked gets into Paula. She turns away and sets her eyes on the glazed horizon where the lake's mouth spreads. She pretends she has not seen Maudie, has not heard her, has not understood that the child has followed her mother and is struggling with her skate laces, too late and slow and clumsy to catch up. A mean wind cuts across the ice. It's too cold to stand still, Paula tells herself. Her weight tilts, her skate glides, she begins to move.

A cry tears out of Maudie and follows her. This time she doesn't call for her mother. It is just a scream. Maybe she took off her gloves, thinks Paula. Maybe the metal of the skate blade has stuck to her fingers. She won't have fastened her cap. Her ears. She'll get frostbite. She slows, turns as if she's only been practising a circle, and skates back to Maudie.

Maudie is crying. Her mouth is open and she has not fastened her new red cap. Her fingers fumble as she sobs. She can't see to do up her skates. Paula looks at the smeared, teary face and frantic fingers, and a wave of love and hate picks her up and throws her far, farther than it has ever thrown her before. She kneels down in front of Maudie and fixes her laces, and then snaps the cap down over Maudie's ears. Maudie has taken off her gloves to do up the skates, just as Paula has always told her she must not. Maudie's fingers get mixed up and slide into the wrong spaces and Paula puts them on.

'Can I – can I come with you?' hiccups Maudie.

'Yes,' says Paula. She is not going back to the cottage with this child.

The two of them step out on to the ice. Maudie is a good skater, like her mother. In the city Paula takes her to classes at the rink. But Maudie shrinks close to her mother at the sight of the huge white lake opening out in front of them.

'Come on,' says Paula, 'skate behind me and I'll keep the wind off you.'

There is no wind but the wind of their passage. Paula skates fast, leaning into the space that offers itself to her. She hears the child behind her and knows Maudie is following, keeping up with her. The low grey sky is heavier than ever today. Surely it is going to snow.

They've never been so far out. Paula glances back and sees the five inlets, five fingers, disappearing into the woods where the cottages are. They are on the open lake where the ferry runs from shore to shore in summer.

'Mind the branch, Maudie!' she calls back, and Maudie swerves in her mother's blade marks. The branch is frozen into the ice, sticking up a fist of wood. Paula skates faster. She is warm now, her legs moving easily, her arms tingling with life. She could skate like this for hours.

'Mother!' calls Maudie. Paula slows, turns, circles Maudie.

'What is it?'

'Mother, where are we?'

'Why, we're on the lake. Out on the lake where we take the boat.'

Maudie looks round, skating beside her mother now, glancing at the low black line of the shore and the huge nothing between her and home.

'I like it here,' she offers, looking up at her mother's face.

'Do you?' says Paula, but she looks out, way away from

Maudie, smiling, and so she doesn't see the tip of Maudie's left skate catch on a rough place in the ice, and Maudie hang for a second at awkward half-stretch and then crash down on the ice. But she hears it. She is with Maudie in a second. Maudie is white, cawing from the bottom of her chest. Her breath has been knocked out of her. Paula gets her up, sits her, supports her while Maudie fights to breathe. She mustn't sit on the ice, thinks Paula, she will freeze. Maudie's nostrils spread wide, reaching for air. The first breath Maudie gets she uses to cry. Paula holds her, Maudie with her heavy little skates dangling, her red cap twisted sideways, her cheek beginning to ooze reddish purple blood.

'It's OK, baby,' says Paula, hoisting Maudie higher. 'Show me where it hurts now.' But Maudie cries and scrubs her face against her mother, clinging to her with her legs so the sharp blades dig through Paula's ski-trousers.

'Come on, birdie,' says Paula, 'show me your face. Come on, bird-spice.' She hasn't called Maudie that for years. Why did she think of it? The snowsuit is so bulky she can scarcely feel Maudie through it. No broken bones, though. She is frightened, not hurt.

'Maudie,' she says, 'Maudie. You've got to be a big girl now. Look around.' Maudie puts her head out and peeps over the puffy horizon of Paula's snowsuit shoulder.

'We have to get back,' says Paula.

'Carry me,' says Maudie.

'I can't,' says Paula. 'Not that far.' She feels Maudie let her body go floppy in her mother's arms. She looks down. Maudie has shut her eyes tight, the way she does when she wants to be carried upstairs to bed. Eric always carries her in the end, after Maudie's begged and pleaded and pretended to be asleep.

'No,' says Paula quietly, 'this is real, Maudie. You have to skate.'

Maudie doesn't understand, she knows. She is a city child, not like Paula, who grew up here and always knew that winter was hungry, just waiting for you to make a mistake. It got someone every year. Hunting accidents, frostbite, a boy skating too late into the spring. Maudie doesn't know about any of that. Why should she? They're summer and Christmas visitors with a car-full of things from the city.

But Maudie understands a certain tone in her mother's voice. She lets Paula put her down on the ice and brush off her snowsuit.

'Take my hand,' says Paula.

They skate slowly, side by side. Maudie is pale. She puts her head down against the bitter air which cuts into her face.

'I'll look out for both of us,' promises Paula. She scans the ice for branches, stones, rough places which might catch Maudie's skates. They have come a long way out, much farther than she thought. She sees something dark on the ice, swerves, stops.

'It's a bird,' says Maudie. 'What's the matter with it?'

The bird is dead, lying on its back, its claws hooked. It is perfect. Nothing has touched it.

'It must have just fallen,' says Paula. 'It wasn't here before. Look, this is the way we came, you can see our skate marks.'

'Why did it die?' asks Maudie.

'I don't know. I expect it just froze. You know what Mrs Svendson said, about the birds in her yard?'

Maudie puts out her hand and touches the bird. It is already hard, its eyes open but shrouded. She picks it up and holds it flat on the palm of her glove. Wind ruffles back its feathers.

'It's a redwing,' says Paula, 'see,' and she shows Maudie the markings.

'It just fell out of the air,' says Maudie. She has forgotten her own fall.

'Yes, I think so.'

'How fast did it fall?'

'Not very fast. It isn't hurt.'

Maudie looks up, as if to see a sky drifting with the slow fall of birds. She pats the redwing again.

'Can we bury it? Can we make it a little grave?'

'No, Maudie. We can't skate all that way back carrying it.'

'But if we leave it here, an animal's going to eat it.'

'That's OK, Maudie. It'll just stay here in the quiet. That's what happens to birds when they die. And when it snows it'll cover up the bird like a blanket all winter.'

Maudie puts her face close to the bird's beak and frozen eyes.

'He wants to stay here,' she says finally, and she lays it down on the ice.

'Good girl,' says Paula. 'Now let's go.'

When they reach the shore Maudie is too stiff even to sit and have her skates taken off. Paula lifts her, skates and all, and lugs her up the slope through the trees to the cottage. The lights are on. Suddenly they spring out, marking the ground and making it dark where Paula and Maudie come up the track.

'I bet they're still playing with Kay's Gameboy,' says Maudie. 'He won't ever let me play.'

'Oh well,' says Paula, 'he only had it today.'

'Yeah,' says Maudie. 'Anyway, Kay didn't go out on the ice. None of us've ever been that far before, have we?'

'No.'

'You and me are the only ones who got to do it,' says Maudie. 'Next Christmas I won't fall over. We'll skate all the way. Right down the lake. Can we?'

'Yeah,' says Paula, 'if you still want to.'

They go in and shut the door. That night, in the dark when Maudie and Paula are asleep, it starts to snow.

Short Days, Long Nights

By her right ear an accordion gnaws at the first bars of a song. A voice comes in singing nasally and complacently to itself, so faraway, so sad and so saleable that her eyes fill at once with responsive tears:

> *I build a house for my love*
> *in the dark forest,*
> *I take her away*
> *when winter comes,*
>
> *we sleep together*
> *while the snow falls on us*
> *and when the snow melts*
> *no one will find us . . .*

She must have left the radio on all night. It sounds terrible. She'll have to get new batteries at the kiosk, first thing. She rolls over, humping the sheet and the quilt. Above the bed there's a notice-board with lists pinned to it. She scribbles BATTERIES under MORE THINGS TO DO.

She flops back, but not without seeing that there is some-one else in the bed. Someone else in the bed. Well. She'll just let her thoughts take a walk, she thinks. Grey light drips round the blinds, not getting far. But it was worth spending so much money on this hand-made, low, slatted pine bed with its thick mattress which is so well sprung that you can't tell by the give in it that there is anybody else in the bed. In her old bed they'd have bumped into one another long before morning.

– A man, she supposes cautiously. The quilt is flounced up round his ears so you can't tell. It could be one of her women friends who didn't have enough money for a taxi?

'No, you mustn't walk back on your own. Come and sleep at my place. I've got an enormous bed now.'

Can she remember any conversation like that? She sifts and searches but there's nothing there at all. A white-out. And yet she doesn't feel bad. In fact she feels wonderful: light and warm and energetic as if a secret fuel has been streaming into her all through the hours of her sleep. This is the kind of mood when she'll do half-forgotten ballet exercises for forty minutes before slicing herself a plateful of black bread and Swiss cheese and eating it in the bath.

She shifts her head from side to side. Not a trace of head-ache, and no nausea. And she knows this is not the fragile, hallucinatory absence of hangover which comes when you're still actually drunk from the night before: the sort which throws you to the ground, gasping for Vichy water and aspi-rin, as soon as you bend over to pull up your tights.

He's having a terrific sleep, that's for sure. He's on his stomach, and his heels make a bump in the quilt way down the bed. He's tall. She stretches her body down, comparing their heights. He has black hair pushed up at the back by the quilt. Little damp sweaty feathers of it stick up at the crown of his head. She takes a pinch of hair and rubs it between her finger and thumb. Its soft sooty black ought to come off on her hand. She eases the quilt away from the back of his neck very gently, so that the colder air won't wake him, and peers down the tunnel at his body. His shoulders are still brown, although it's January. Perhaps he's just come back from a winter holiday in Tunisia. His skin has a light cereal smell – nice. She lifts the quilt higher and sights the moony glow of his buttocks. He twitches and she drops the quilt back on him with a slight hoosh of escaping air.

From the back at least, he looks fine. She moves her own body about in the bed, listening for anything it can tell her. Stickiness, aches, chafings? It would be as well to sort out what's been going on before he wakes up. But she isn't getting any signals. Her body feels dry and whole and sweet-tempered. Her foot brushes a piece of cloth and she draws it up, clenched between her toes. A neat, clean pair of French navy Y-fronts. Not a style she likes, but expensive. With three brothers, she's an expert on men's underpants. They used to leave them lying all over the house, dirty ones with skids on them lying on the top of the stairs when her father and mother had friends in to supper.

She gets out of bed without sending the slightest tremor through the body on her left side, and pads over the matting to the window. Thick whirling funnels of snow come at her. The outer window is furred. She smiles. She must have slept for hours – no wonder she feels so good. It's ten to eleven. The kiosk opposite is lit up and the doughnut stall down the road is wreathed in steam. Nobody much about, though, on a Sunday morning like this. The snow plough tramps steadily down to the Kauppatori and back, banking soft fresh new snow over the dirty packed ice of last week's fall. There's so much that there'll be lorries coming soon to cart it away, on to the wasteland.

The thought of an apple doughnut makes her mouth tingle. A long satchel of sugary dough, a tongueful of apple. She could dive out now and bring back one for each of them. Or perhaps he's one of those men who'd eat sausage first thing in the morning, with plenty of sharp, watery pickles on it? She could get the batteries, and some cigarettes, too.

She pulls on a long warm vest that's been flung down on a chair. It smells slightly of yesterday. She finds clean pants and a pair of jeans and puts them on, then she combs out her hair and plaits it tightly so that it won't blow out across her face in the snowstorm. She shakes an empty cigarette pack out of her leather jacket, and puts the jacket on.

One of his hands has fallen loose from the quilt, and dangles off the low bed. Its back brushes the floor. There are more soft dark hairs on the hand and the forearm. Somehow the hand is familiar to her in a way the rest of the body is not. She can picture it lifting a glass, taking a cigarette. The hand must have been somewhere off to the side of her field of vision the evening before. It is certainly not the hand of the man she drank with and danced with. She has a face to go with that one. She concentrates, but it's impossible. She can't locate a man to go with the dangling hand.

But all the same it is sad to see a hand hanging out of her bed. She kneels down beside it and slides her own hand underneath it, scooping it off the floor. Now the full weight of the hand lies in her own. It's quite cool. The straw-scented heat she's smelled around his body hasn't got down this far.

She bends one of the fingers a little and it stays bent, just as she has arranged it. She straightens it again. Then she leans over and breathes into the palm, in and out, again, again, until the moisture of her breath gathers on his skin. She lifts the hand to her own face and lays it against her cheek. Very lightly she begins to caress it, with her cheek, with her lips, with her tongue. With her teeth she nips off one of the soft black hairs, then she wipes the hand very gently of her breath and her spit, and lays it back on the mattress, along the man's bare side, with its palm still upturned. She draws the light, dense quilt right over it. Then she crosses to the window and pulls down the string of the Venetian blinds.

In less than three hours' time it'll be dark again.

The Bridge Painter

I'm used to the wind. That's the first question people ask. Don't you get blown about all the time? Doesn't your stuff get blown away?

Over the years you learn. I keep my hair short. I wear wool. There's nothing worse than denim when the wind sets in from the north-east, with grains of ice in it. Some languages, they have a hundred words for snow. Wet snow, snow that's melted then frozen over, snow that's soft and new and just clinging together. They have a word for every type. But of course you only get the language you need. That's why there's fewer and fewer people I feel like talking to these days. 'Bit chilly,' they say, on their five-minute dash down to the paper shop in their slippers. They don't even look at the sky, not properly. Weather's nothing to them. They take a fug of indoors with them wherever they go.

And when it comes to waterproofs I don't skimp. If you spend all the hours of daylight outdoors, winter and summer, then it's worth any money to be dry and warm. I go for the new, breathable fabrics, the ones that don't trap your sweat in a cold slick next to you. Ninety-six quid this anorak cost me. No, you'd never believe it.

Ah. You've guessed it. Or you're beginning to. Why's he paying for his own gear, if he's a bridge painter? Don't the contractors supply protective clothing? What's all this about paying ninety-six quid for an anorak? You're on the right track. We'll get there.

I'm on the second Severn crossing now. I've done the first, of course. Many, many times. Back when it was just an idea walking on stilts, then time after time with the traffic pouring over it like it was a street in the sky. It *is* a street in the sky. That's what I like. The shapes. The rush. The cornflakes lorry bounding over the bridge with the great big shine of the estuary behind it. I can guess how big a pock each lorry would make in the mud, if it fell. But it's never going to fall. That's what these bridges are all about.

The second Severn crossing's coming along nicely. Not long now till there are the two of them stitching up the big gape of water and air, like two smiles. What I need now is an aerial view. A light plane. I'll do it one day. It's lucky most people don't realize that if you really want one thing and dedicate yourself to it, you're more or less sure to get it.

Like I've dedicated myself to bridges. The place where I am now, this particular journey, is all part of it. I've come to see the new bridge they're building between Fyn and Sjaelland. That's in Denmark. The bridge goes seventeen kilometres between the two islands. It has to put its foot down once, but that's all it does to span all that space. It's the biggest this and the longest that. But a bridge is just a noise in my head until I see it. I've been everywhere. There's nowhere I won't go to paint a bridge. Nothing I won't do. No, I mean that.

So here I am in Denmark, on the ferry that does the job that the bridge'll do once it's built. It's a nice ferry, top of the range, like a big tea-tray gliding over the sea. It's got no idea at all that it's about to become obsolete. Not that it's going out of service: for political reasons, I suppose, they'll keep it on. Most of the passengers stay in the train down below. They're so used to the journey they don't even bother to register the change from land to water by getting out of their seats. Those that *have* bothered are glumly shovelling in pastries in the cafeteria. They don't care what the bridge is doing.

It's a bright blue day up here. No wonder our tea-tray's gliding along so smoothly. You could stroke this water. Not a breath of wind. Only the churn of our engines. But I'm on the wrong side of the ferry. I'll have to make haste, because we only stay on it an hour.

And there she is. Up on her legs but not walking yet. A beautiful baby. What a bridge she's going to be. Great pillars standing in the middle of bright blue nothing. And on the top of them, cranes that look like flies with one leg hooked up. It brings tears to my eyes. No, it does, truly. I shut my eyes and I can almost see the curve of the earth with pillars marching across it.

And the winds. The crosswinds. The thwack of wind all winter long. That's what she's going to take, what she's been born for. Wind and weight and weather. But she stands there, making herself ready. And then she'll step away.

The thing about a bridge, it's never afraid. It's built to take the stress. Built to give. Not like a human being.

'It is causing a lot of trouble, that bridge.'

I didn't see her come up, but here she is at my elbow, crowding out my view. No chance of standing still and staring. They all speak English better than I do.

'Oh? How's that then?' I wait for her to tell me about the inevitable construction problems. Delays, deaths. Don't they know that's what has to happen, with a bridge?

'Many people don't want it. It will change things. Change our country. Lorries will come up through Germany, over to Copenhagen, on to Sweden. Everything will be different.'

And about bloody time too, I think, but I don't say it. They should think themselves lucky. They don't know what bridges cost. Years ago they knew the price and they paid it. '*London Bridge is falling down, falling down, falling down . . .*' Nice little rhyme. What it's really about, is human sacrifice. '*Set a watchman to watch all night, watch all night, watch all night . . .*' They've found watchmen, lodged in some of these old bridges. Little curled-up skeletons. Cats, or children. Wall them in and they become watchmen. They keep the bridge safe, keep it standing. For it's hard to keep a bridge standing above the swirl of water, what with the weight and the wind and weather. So they set a watchman. It's what they thought a bridge needed, then. Or wanted, perhaps.

I let the Danish woman clatter on about ecological opposition for a bit, while I make my first sketches, sizing up the huge pale tan column riding against an island. It's the first touch I like. Knowing how well I'm going to come to know her. All I have with me today is my sketchbook and pack of pencils. It's the first touch, the first line now. All that whiteness of paper takes shape once you make a mark on it. The Danish woman's watching but that doesn't stop me. She'll get fed up soon, wander off. They always do.

A bridge like this, you can't hurry her. Yes, I'll give her all the time she wants. That woman's too close. Pecking her head in at my sketch like a hen. Peck away. You'll find you're pecking at stone. There's nothing for you here. No lovely view, no nice little clouds and waves. Just the bridge.

The bridge is real. The land is only an idea. Call it England, call it Wales. Whatever you call it you can't make it any different. It stays where it is, as it is. But a bridge does things. A bridge is alive.

I'm going to tell you something you may not want to know. But I'll turn the page first. There. All that excitement every time and then the first sketch is never any good. It doesn't matter. You have to do it, to get on to the next one. I tear off the sheet, crumple it into a ball and toss it into the sea. The Danish woman looks at me. I've really shown myself up now. Go on, leave me alone, leave me alone. Get down below to your coffee and cake.

And she does. I make a mark on my second sheet. You monster, you beautiful monster. If you put your foot down on this ferry you'd send us straight to the bottom. All those little lives working on you, serving you. You deserve it. You're going to be so beautiful. They can't stop you now, not the environmental campaigners, not the economists, not the local politicians nor the big guns in government. They've got more than they bargained for, building you.

'*Set a watchman to watch all night, watch all night, watch all night.*' I've done that too. There, that made you jump. I'm not just a bridge painter. What next? What's he going to tell us next? Are we going to have to do something about him?

Not if you don't want to. Don't get worried. Listen. I first got the idea fifteen years ago. It was just a little bridge over the River Rye. There'd always been a bridge there, but none of them lasted that long. Sticks and stones, bricks, rubble, cement: over the centuries they'd tried the lot. But it was a fast, thin, wicked little river just there, and it ate away the piles and shook the arches every time it flooded. They were stripping it down and rebuilding it.

It was evening, about eight o'clock. One of those green dusks you get near rivers, and the midges were biting. I was sitting there, sketching a pile of stones they'd pulled down and set aside for the rebuilding. That was when she came. She had her baby in one of those slings. They weren't so common then. And he'd fallen asleep.

'It's late for him to be out,' she said, 'but he's been driving me mad crying all day. It's the only way I can get a bit of peace.' She was about seventeen I should say. No wedding ring. Meagre little face with big startled eyes. Peace, I thought, I'll give you peace. I kept on sketching. The light was going fast.

It's very quiet just there. Mostly a bridge brings houses and people, but over the years the flooding had driven the village away, up on to higher ground. The baby's cheek pressed against the side of the sling. I remember thinking there'd be a mark. Fast asleep, eaten up with sleep. The girl looked up and down the path, then at my sketch. No one but us for half a mile or more. She touched the baby's cheek with the back of a finger, but he didn't stir.

That's when I had my idea. I remembered those little curled skeletons they'd dug out from among the stones. They were never far from my mind. At odd times I'd think of hands reaching into the dark to place the baby inside. Then other hands knocking the stones into place. I could see it all.

'You drawing that bridge?' she asked.

'What does it look like?' I said. I looked at the heap of stones, and then at the baby. My idea grew strong.

Don't be frightened. It's not what you think. About the same time they brought in those slings, they brought in dolls that really looked like babies, dolls you could change and cuddle and stick a bottle into, with the same squashed face as a real baby. A few feet away, you can't tell them from the real thing.

I can't tell you how many granddaughters I must have by now. Every time I go into the shop it's the same. 'One of those real baby dolls. Yes, the one that cries. For my granddaughter.'

Or these days, with self-service, I don't even need to ask.

There's always a time when the men are off-site. I'm a bit of a bricklayer now, as well as a painter. Or sometimes I just dig a hole at the foot of the pile nearest the water. No one's ever seen me. And I set a watchman to watch all night. Curl it up, with its thumb in its mouth. It'll last for ever, with these modern materials. As long as the bridge does. The little soft babyface lying in the dark. You can't ask a bridge what it wants, but if you've a feeling for it, you know without words. All over the country I've been, and beyond. Painting the bridges, and setting watchmen for them. It's only what they deserve. When I die I'll leave a nursery of my babies underground.

So now you know what's in the parcel I'm putting into the big pocket of my waterproof. It's soft, squashy, and not very heavy. I've finished my sketch. In three minutes, according to my calculations, we'll be as close to the bridge as this ferry goes. That woman's gone below and there's nothing but me and the bright blue sky. And the bridge.

But you can't dig a hole in the sea. No, I know that. And it's no good unless you hide away your watchman in the dark with your own hands. My hands are ready. I watch them grip the rail where it's cold and slippery. I notice, as if they're someone else's hands, how rough they are, how chapped from years of working in the open air. Then they tense, taking my weight, ready to climb. I shall set my watchman. The sea's so smooth, so flat you could almost believe you could walk on it.

Spring Wedding

'Oh God, I don't know what's the matter,' groans Jorma. His pale fluffy cheek vibrates against hers. He's crying.

No he's not. The second she peeks up, timid with concern, he throws himself back on to her and they roll over in his narrow pine bed until Ulli's head and shoulders are tipping dangerously over the edge and Jorma has to haul her back on to the mattress. The quilt slides off on to the floor. The room's warm, but even so Ulli feels exposed. If he wants to, Jorma can see all of her. She had kept her baggy T-shirt on as she ducked under the quilt, and then somehow it had got rolled up over her head and now it's lying in a ball in the corner of the room. Jorma's bedroom. Jorma's lucky. His father is an architect and he's made a huge low room up here for his two sons, with wide, sweet-smelling, pine-planked floor and pine-panelled walls. A blond room, cupping light even when it's grey outside. A steep window set in the roof, and a long desk underneath it, for Jorma and Jussi to study.

Jorma has the room to himself this weekend. His parents and his brother are away at a family wedding, but Jorma's got out of it because he has a test coming up on the Monday, an important test in English and Maths for which he'll be able to revise in the peace and quiet of the empty house. Can his parents really believe one word of it, Ulli asks herself. She doesn't know what to make of Jorma's parents. They are effusive on the telephone, ostentatiously welcoming when she comes to their house to listen to music and drink coffee upstairs with Jorma and Jussi. They have managed to let her know that Jorma has lots of little girlfriends who are always ringing up or calling round, and that while of course they're perfectly happy about that, it's rather hard for his parents to tell one little girl from the next.

One time they'd had friends round for drinks when she'd been there. Jorma's mother had insisted on introducing Ulli to everybody, even though Jorma had clearly been trying to edge her past the open sitting-room door and up the stairs without attracting anybody's attention. Ulli had come on her bike and she was out of breath and conscious of sweaty hands. She had her jeans on, and a sweatshirt which she'd tie-dyed unsuccessfully. Jorma's parents and their friends were dressed in expensive buff and white and cream playclothes that cuffed the women's carefully waxed legs. Jorma's mother had a plain gold chain round her neck. She wore a yellow linen dress and shoes of soft peach-coloured leather, and her pale hair was coiled into a knot at the back of her neck. Not one wisp slipped loose.

'Did you do this yourself?' she asked, fingering Ulli's sweatshirt. 'That's marvellous, isn't it, darling? You young people are so creative.'

Beside Ulli, Jorma scowled and darkened. 'It's not a work of art, Mummy. You don't have to make such a thing about it.'

His mother slid her eyes sideways towards her guests in mock despair. Her fingers touched Jorma's cheek coolly, lightly.

'What about that revision, darling? I'm sure Ulli's got work to do as well. I don't want to get in your parents' bad books for letting Jorma distract you from your studies, Ulli.'

'You don't need to worry about Ulli, Mummy. She's about a million times brighter than me, ask anyone. And she's got two more years ahead of her.'

'Gracious, Ulli, are you only sixteen? I'd never have thought it. Your face is quite . . . old . . . somehow.'

There was a silence, and then, 'Oh well, off you go. But don't forget, darling, the Manners will be here at six. And I particularly want you to look after Maija-Liisa. She's such a lovely girl, but so shy.'

'I must admit,' cut in Jorma's father bluffly, 'I rather like to see that in a young girl.'

Ulli shuts her mind. It's all in the past and anyway Jorma's parents are a hundred kilometres away, drinking champagne or whatever people drink at weddings these days. Triple schnapps, if the colour of Jorma's father's face is anything to go by. He doesn't like Ulli. His dislike makes her skin stiffen and prickle when she has to pass him on the stairs.

Jorma is rubbing his thumb up and down the inside curve of her hip-bone. Her stomach lies slack and shallow. She feels she's scarcely breathing. Jorma lays his head on her stomach, and shuts his eyes.

'I can hear your stomach rumbling,' he says. 'Just think, I know more about what's going on inside you than you do.'

His head is very heavy. Now she believes what she has learned at school about the relative weight of the head to the rest of the body. His hair is so soft and fine, and yet it curls. She can unroll one of the curls, and he doesn't even notice. He's as good as asleep, and she doesn't want to disturb him, but she's starving. She thinks of the big white double-doored fridge in the kitchen/breakfast-room downstairs. There's always enough juice in Jorma's house, in glass pitchers without smears or streaks on them. There are fruit yoghurts in packs of a dozen, and iced buttermilk to drink. Jorma's mother doesn't go to the market. She buys fruit the expensive way, in the supermarket, and it lies in the fridge solid and clean in its plastic wrappers, unbruised, giving off no scent. Ulli dreams of a cheese sandwich. The lurch of her stomach juices stirs Jorma, and she tips him off her and folds her body away from his. She doesn't want to walk away with her back to him. She will feel him looking at her. She dives, scoops up the white baggy T-shirt and pulls it over her head. She shakes out her hair over it. Jorma is leaning up on one elbow, resting on his side and looking at her. His face is wiped clean with sleep, its strong irregular bones softened.

'. . . about a million times brighter than me . . .'

No. It isn't so. His green eyes clear and look at her. He isn't smiling, but his face brims with willingness to smile. He's waiting for her to tuck up her feet under the T-shirt and sit facing him on the other end of the bed. She is studying Baudelaire and he likes her to recite the poems to him in French. He dropped French way back, when he was fourteen. There didn't seem any point in his going on, all the teachers had agreed. Even the private tutor his mother got hold of didn't do the trick. It was just like eating something that disagreed with him. But Ulli knows that put Jorma in a café in a little French seaside town where they don't speak a word of any other language, and he'd come back half an hour later knowing that there's a little beach near by you can get to if you go round the rocks at low tide – it's always deserted and you can swim with nothing on . . .

'J'aime de vos longs yeux la lumière verdâtre . . .'

she begins. He nods and closes his eyes.

38

'Don't you want to know what it means?' she asks.

'Not really. It's the sound I like. The sound of your voice. You know, I used to hate French at school, but it's nice when you speak it.'

'Don't you wish we could go there? To France, I mean?'

'No, why? I like this.'

'Do you? What about this?'

She puts out a foot and stirs his ribs.

'Listen. Don't go falling asleep again. Listen to this one and tell me if it doesn't make you want to go far away, as far away as you possibly can.

> *'Mon enfant, ma soeur*
> *Songe à la douceur*
> *D'aller là-bas vivre ensemble . . .'*

'I suppose it might, if I could understand it,' says Jorma. 'Was there something about a sister? *J'ai une soeur et un frère.* My tutor was always on at me to say that for some reason. Why is it that when you're learning a foreign language, you always have to tell lies?'

He catches hold of her foot and holds it for a moment, looking at the structure of her toes and the tan marks from her sandals. They're still there, the marks of last summer's sun, even after the long winter when her foot's been sheathed in her brown leather boots with their sheepskin lining. At this time of year Ulli finds it hard to remember what sun feels like on bare skin. It's mid-April. Two weeks now since she stopped being a virgin. Funny how often she's thought of it that way, since it happened. She can't remember thinking of herself as a virgin beforehand. But now she thinks of it and says it over and over in her mind, in the long quiet sunlit classroom during her Maths test, or when she's gulping down coffee before she catches the bus to school. The word feels like a splinter deep inside her, not a splinter of ice but something quick and hot and alive. She's getting to love the word virgin. Virgin. Non-virgin.

Words in a changing-room:

'Technically, I'm sure I'm not a virgin any more.'

'No, it's all right if you do that. You're still a virgin really. Otherwise nobody'd be a virgin if they used tampons, would they?'

'My mother still won't let me use tampons. She says they give you cancer.'

My child, my sister . . .

Jorma gives the foot back to her and says, 'Come back to bed.'

'I can't, I'm starving.'

'Poke around under the bed. There might be some biscuits. Jussi's always leaving stuff around.'

Jorma puts his lips against the inside of her shoulder, just above the crease of her armpit. He kisses and sips.

'Wouldn't it be nice,' he says, 'if a sort of dew came out all over you. Ulli-dew.'

'Do you know, some people rub margarine all over themselves when they're in bed together,' says Ulli. 'I just can't see why they do it, can you?'

'There's some massage oil in Mummy's bathroom. But I think that's for older people. You know. Their skin's not as nice as yours.'

'What does it taste of?'

'Mmm. I don't know really. Not anything sweet. More like moss, I think.'

'Moss!'

'Mm. More or less. But that's not quite right. It's a bit almondy as well. You know, I could tell it was you anywhere. Even if I had my eyes shut and you were in a room with twenty other people.'

'And you went round and licked them all.'

Jorma's lips move up the shallow curve of Ulli's right breast. She tenses and pulls away from him a little. He looks up. She sees him like a diver coming up out of deep water, his face pale, the pupils of his eyes shrinking as she looks at them.

'What's the matter?'

'Nothing,' says Ulli. 'It wasn't anything really, it's only . . . I wish my breasts were bigger.'

She's never said this to anyone. At school people envy her, or say that they do, because she's slim and can eat what she likes without getting fat. Girls with big breasts hate sports. Their breasts jounce under their light T-shirts and their soft thighs chafe in their shorts. Ulli thinks they look beautiful in the showers, but they'd never believe it.

'But you wouldn't look right if they were,' Jorma says, tracing the line of her breast. Her nipple stiffens. 'Look, the way you are, you balance.'

> *We have a little sister, she has no breasts.*
> *What shall we do for our sister*
> *on the day she is spoken for?*

In Ulli's Bible the Song of Songs is headed over each column of verse:
THE CHURCH PROFESSES HER FAITH: BEAUTY OF THE CHURCH: CHRIST AWAKENS THE CHURCH. She'd turned over the pages one day,

reading the headings, then her eyes had fallen on the words below them. It was a like a punch in the stomach. She had no breath. She could hear the voices speaking and answering one another, as alive as herself, wanting what she wanted.

Now she soaks in what Jorma's just said. She won't think of it now. She'll save it for later on, as she's saved the word virgin, to think about when she's alone.

Look, the way you are, you balance.

The light of a midsummer dawn lies across the bathroom. It breaks on the panel of sea-green glass Mother bought for Pappy on their fifteenth wedding anniversary. Thick sea-green glass with a pattern in it which varies according to where you stand. Ulli was six that year. Mother had told her in secret a few days beforehand, and had shown her the pane of glass, unwrapping a corner of the padded wrapping in its presentation box. The next morning Pappy was shaving and Ulli was watching his face in the mirror when a longing to tell him what his present was began to swell in her until it was so sweet and powerful that her mouth was watering with the words that she knew and he did not. Nothing else mattered. Watching in the mirror she steered mirror-Ulli and mirror-Pappy until they were touching, then she whispered the secret into his elbow.

And after all that Pappy had fitted the pane of glass into the bathroom window, which wasn't at all what Mother was hoping for. She wanted it to be where people would notice it and say how unusual and beautiful it was, and ask her where she had bought it.

'Funny sort of anniversary present, glass,' Pappy had said, as if to himself. 'Risky, I'd have thought. After all, breaking glass is a bad omen.'

'There are some people you just can't please no matter what you do for them,' her mother returned. 'You may not be able to see it, but it's beautiful, isn't it, Ulli?'

The light of a summer dawn spreads itself across the ruck of towels, the split tube of toothpaste, the brushes with hairs in them, the dirty-linen basket. Even though all the boys have left home, there seems to be just as much mess. Nobody has the heart to tidy up, and things lie about where they've been put or dropped until at last one member of the remaining family whirls round with a plastic bin-liner and throws everything in, ready or not. Ulli has taken to cleaning the shower before she gets into it.

Ulli lays a couple of sheets of soft absorbent toilet paper across the toilet bowl, and sits down to pee as quietly as she can. This is the second time she's had to get up tonight, and her mother is restless, coughing and occasionally groaning aloud in the bedroom which is just across from the bathroom door. And the walls are thin. This house is not architect-built. Ulli won't flush the toilet this time.

It's completely light now, and Ulli looks at the watch which she's taken to keeping on all night this past two or three weeks, since she started waking first once and then twice or even three times between going to bed and the official start of the morning at about quarter to seven. It's just gone one. She looks at herself in the big spotted mirror over the basin. She has always loved this mirror, with its secretive look of knowing another country which lies just behind the one it is forced to reflect back at her. She leans in, looks close. Yes, she looks different. There's a shadowy filling out around her jaw. Her eyes are puffy and they have light brown stains under them. Well, of course, she hasn't had any proper sleep for nights and nights. What can you expect. Quickly, she lists to herself everything which accounts for the change in the way she looks. She's tired out. Term only finished last Friday, and it was test after test for weeks beforehand. She hasn't felt like eating much, either. It's the season of midsummer, when usually she'd be making plans with her friends every evening, for barbecues, for trips to the beach, for long evenings with their tanned legs sprawled on the grass, long evenings sitting close to the boys they've discussed endlessly while having their showers and doing their hair beforehand. Sitting closer and closer, nearly touching . . .

But this year it's all different. She has Jorma, and Jorma's away, working as a counsellor in a summer camp two hundred kilometres to the east. It's been fixed up for ages, since long before Ulli and Jorma got together. And he certainly can't cancel now, and let everybody down, his parents are quite definite about that. Besides, Ulli knows that really he doesn't want to. He's worked there before; he knows the kids and they have a great time.

'They're terrific kids, Ulli!'

And it's a kind of social responsibility too. These kids wouldn't have any summer at all, without the camp. Jorma's mother has been careful to explain all this to Ulli. There's a taste of tin in Ulli's mouth. She looks down at her watch. One-fifteen. She ought to go back and try to get some rest, even if she can't sleep. If only she could sleep properly, she's sure she would get rid of the feeling that nothing matters except curling up with her arms around her breasts and stomach, which seem to be tender and aching all over . . .

She stares deep into the mirror again, then with a decisive tug she sweeps the big yellow T-shirt she sleeps in up and over her head, and stands there naked. No, she can't deny it any longer. Her nipples are dark and soft. Her breasts are bigger.

No Jorma here to whisper to. No Jorma to tell her it's nonsense, she's imagining things. No Jorma to wrap her around with himself so that it doesn't seem to matter any more what's true and what isn't, because the rest of the world is floating off somewhere with its dates and deadlines suspended. But the mirror just hangs there, waiting for more. What hasn't it seen? Things Ulli can't even begin to dream of.

'You'll have to try harder than this, if you want to impress me,' says the mirror, 'my child, my sister . . .'

Annina

That time when I was having Annina. The time I had Annina. No. It doesn't sound right. I can say: the time when I was having Blaise. In fact I have said it, often. It's my time, my experience, my possession. No one can contradict me about it.

Long ago in the middle of the night when everyone was sleeping and there was a frost on the ground which killed the last of my geraniums even though they'd lived through the whole of a mild winter, Annina was born.

It doesn't matter what I write, it comes out as lies. And that's very suitable for the story of Annina. Annina's taught me a new language entirely, one of lies and things you leave out. Without it, now, I wouldn't survive. It's more necessary to me than air to breathe.

Annina is my little girl. Annina is my language. I speak Annina. Even in quite ordinary conversations, I pick up scraps of Annina. Out of the fuzz of static which is what ordinary English has become for me, I catch a phrase. Annina.

> *My little baby-waby*
> *My drop of honey*
> *My own, my secret one.*

Quite often I hear lovers speaking a bit of Annina. It may be nauseating, but by God it's recognizable, like one of those tunes you just hear once and it happens that you've got a new dress on and the sun's shining so warmly you can smell both the cotton and your own skin.

But this isn't doing you justice, Annina. Here I am making a mystery out of you when all you ever wanted was to be a secret, and you're that for sure now, because even if I wanted to pick you up and brandish you for the world to see, you've gone. The traces you've left are only those that might be made by any sick-hearted woman whose son has grown up and gone, a woman who's always wanted a little girl, but whose little girl would need to be more a doll than a thing of flesh. THING. I never called you that. I did Blaise, of course.

'Come here, you bad thing, wait till Mummy catches you.'
None of that with Annina.
'My daughter', I called her, and 'my girl'.
Never little. Never creature. Never thing.

Annina was not quite small enough to sleep inside a walnut shell. The cracked shell of a hard-boiled egg, for sure, but that would have been unnecessary. It was easy enough to make things nice for her, and why shouldn't she have her own bed with pillow and sheets and quilt like any Christian? And she was a Christian, I made sure of that. The big drop of holy water swelling and breaking across her face. Her mouth squaring with anger. And I made the sign of the cross without bruising her forehead. I wasn't sure if I'd done it right, so I went to an old Jesuit in a church in the city centre and told him what I'd done; nothing about the size of Annina, for fear he'd write me off as a madwoman, but everything else.

Though maybe I could have told him, for he looked as if nothing in the world would surprise him. I'd done right, it seemed. But as I came out and felt Annina stir in her quilted sling under my blouse, I wondered why it had seemed to matter so much and why I'd gone running to the priest when there was Annina, warm and fragile as a new-laid egg. Already, even though she wasn't yet speaking, a bit of Annina's language had got between me and the priest, and somehow it wasn't the word of Annina I doubted. She was always as warm as any other child. I don't know why that should have surprised me, but it did, almost as if I thought she should have had a slighter heat to match her slight size. Or perhaps it was all the stories I used to read in my *Green Fairy Book* and my *Red Fairy Book*, where the fairies were cold and magical and lived under the hills.

But don't mistake me. Annina is no fairy.

Let's go back to when I had Annina, since there doesn't seem to be any more accurate way of putting it. Blaise was eight at the time. He was tall for his age and he'd just had his hair cut short and freckles were coming on his nose and his cheeks from playing out after school with his friends, now the days were growing longer and lighter. He was not my baby any more, but I didn't mind that. I have never wanted to be the sort of woman who stands back, bruised and brave, to let her young hero make his own way in life. And lets him know that she's always waiting for him back at home. Besides, for the first time since Blaise's birth, I was pregnant again. Not far along, about nine weeks. We'd always wanted more children, but since Blaise it'd been as if we were sitting by one of those rivers you know is full of fish, with juicy bait and a good line but not a single bite the whole afternoon. Not that we were that bothered. We'd enjoyed those afternoons, with the sun on us and the water spreading out and the chance of a little fish under the surface. No, we weren't bothered.

So I was looking at my future in a new way when one afternoon just before Blaise came home I bent down to see if the frost really had got the geraniums or not, and when I straightened up there was something warm and wet running down my legs. My first thought was that I'd wet myself. It was a long time since I'd been pregnant and anything seemed possible. But of course it was red and it was blood and at the same time it began to hurt, very slyly, as if it was mocking the period which would have come around that time of the month if I hadn't been pregnant.

And then there were hours of hot panic, with the doctor coming and being sorry but I'd lost the baby, and Matt coming home seeming to bring the noise and smell of the schoolchildren with him, since he'd come out of class so suddenly. Then Matt went downstairs to cook sausages just for Blaise, when he came home. Neither of us felt like anything.

There was a little prickle under the sheet. The first stir of that small heat I grew to know better than my own temperature. Annina.

There was a cord like a cotton thread, so I bit through it. She was an inch and a half long and as fast asleep as if she was only halfway through her long journey, and she was damned if she was going to wake up somewhere dull in the middle of it. Not like Blaise, I thought. Blaise was born crying. And that was the first difference between them which occurred to me.

I wiped the blood off her with a corner of my nightgown, then I got up although I was still bleeding and found a box of fancy handkerchiefs in my top left-hand drawer. They were fine lace and the kind of useless thing you get given and then keep by you for years without using, but they did for Annina.

She looked just like a handkerchief in my hand when Matt came into the room with a cup of tea.

'What are you doing out of bed?' he asked, and set down my cup of tea in a hurry and helped me back to lie down. All the time I held on to Annina in that light way you do when you've got something in your hand which might break, and I prayed that she wouldn't make a sound, though what kind of noise a baby her size might make, I couldn't imagine.

Of course I found out soon enough. That was the first bit of her language Annina taught me. A lighter, croakier sound than I'd thought. If I breathed in hard and groaned as if in my sleep, I could hide her cries with my own breathing. After a couple of months I couldn't breathe any other way when I lay down to sleep. Matt said to me once, gentle and awkward, 'I always knew you minded more than you let on. That was when you began groaning in your sleep.'

Feeding you, Annina! Well, you made it clear right from the start that there was going to be no satisfying you on nectar and honey-dew. Cow's milk, boiled and cooled and strained, a drop at a time from an eye-dropper. But it gave you wind and you cried for two hours one night while I shifted about in bed and wheezed and moaned to cover it. So I asked a friend who'd had a baby born at seven months, just marvelling casually at how well she'd managed and how the little thing had thrived, and she told me they'd fed her on goats' milk right from the beginning, on her midwife's advice since her own milk had dried up after a week.

'Right, that's for you, Annina,' I said to myself, and I told Matt that I was going to drink goats' milk from now on, in the hope of curing an itchy rash I'd got between my fingers. How I hated that stuff! But you loved it. I could swear now that I saw the pink flush through your skin when you had your first feed of it, drop by drop, at blood-heat. I could see your right leg kicking as you swallowed it.

You didn't cry much after that. Often you'd be awake, for I'd feel you moving against me in the little pouch I made for you, hung around my neck and hidden by a loose blouse. Poor Matt missed the way we used to sleep together naked, skin to skin, and make love when we were half awake and half sleeping. I think he believed I'd lost heart for making love now I'd lost the baby, even though he must have known that for me that had never been the point of it. So I made a nest for you under my bed and I would tuck you there until I was sure from Matt's breathing that he was asleep. Then I'd bring you into the bed with me, because otherwise I was afraid you'd cry in the night and I wouldn't hear you. And I was afraid of other things for you: wasps and mice and spiders which would be half the size of you or more. When I started to think of dogs and cats I had to close my mind and tell myself: *Take one step at a time.*

We had no cat or dog ourselves, only a pair of goldfish which were like dolphins in your eyes. Do you remember how I let you swim in the tank with them when you begged me to let you, and the big goldfish hung quite still in the water with terror before he dived into the weed and lay trembling next to the china diver that had got rooted in there over the years? I told you to keep away from the weed, but as usual you paid little attention and swam in and out of it, peeking at me through the side of the tank and no doubt laughing to yourself for the sheer pleasure you were having. Then afterwards you danced naked on your towel till you were dry, clapping your hands. I can still hear your hands, clapping.

The thing was, you were so beautiful. I was always looking for excuses to be alone so that I could open your pouch and look at you curled up there. Anybody could have pinched your life out with a finger, but you lay there so much alive with a life of your own, so much taken up with your own dreams or your full warm stomach or the feel of my skin against your hands that I could never think of you as defenceless.

It's not ordinary beauty I'm talking about, anyway. How could you fail to have fine features, even though you took after me with my red cheeks and my black eyebrows that nearly meet over my nose? Nothing frightened you. You hadn't got a chance, really, if you'd only known it, but you got by because you refused to know it, and often I would just burst out laughing for joy at your boldness. What age do babies learn to climb? I suppose they don't climb a lot, in the usual way, but you climbed everywhere. Up my openwork vest. In and out of my front-fastening bra. And my hair! – you couldn't leave it alone. The day I made a plait and you went up it hand-over-hand until you reached my parting and you were so close to my ear I could hear you breathing hard and egging yourself on. I had a hand cupped under you all the time.

All this time you were reaching out, I was closing myself away. There was a job I would have killed for the year before, playing piano for a music therapist in a unit for handicapped children, but I had to turn it down. You were three by then, and I couldn't trust you to keep out of sight. By four you were learning, and at five I could take you anywhere and you'd lie still against me or I'd feel your body vibrating with laughter as you peered out through the gap in my blouse. What a sight I was! Loose blouses, sensible dresses with collars and plenty of pleats down the front. My sister Claire burst out once:

'For God's sake, Teresa, will you look at yourself in the mirror? It's the middle of July, why don't you put on your shorts and a sun-top like you used to? You're only thirty-one and anybody would think you were forty!' She was quite right. I looked older. Men didn't whistle or call after me in the streets any more as they'd been doing since I was twelve years old. I could wander along with my face up to the sun, and if my lips moved, nobody seemed to pay any attention. I think I must have had that look some women get when they're well on in pregnancy, inward and a bit taken up with something all the time. And that's a look which makes people leave you alone.

Did Matt know about you, or didn't he? Often, again and again, I'd think he'd seen you. I'd think maybe he played with you and talked to you and never let on for fear that once the whole business was out in the open we would have to do something about you. People would come to the house and tell us that arrangements ought to be made for you. You needed protection; a safe place maybe where you could be kept well away from things which would do you harm. Some-where light and clean and airy with a spy-hole so that you could be kept an eye on. A little box for you.

You were ten years old and five inches tall. You ran fast, and you jumped high and when you skipped your feet didn't seem to touch the ground. Size for size, I'm sure you were quicker and nimbler than other children. When I looked closely at your feet I saw how strongly made they were, with high arches and long toes so you could climb and judge a distance and leap without ever making a mistake.

No, of course you made mistakes, Annina. Remember when my worst fear was realized and a cat got into the garden while I had my back turned to you, weeding. And you put out your fist to it and hit it on the nose as hard as you could so that it sprang back and cowered by the bird table, but not without giving you a slash on your forearm which was like a rip in silk. And it wanted stitching, but I couldn't think of anybody I could trust to do it, so I bound it tightly with the edges of the wound together and dressed it every day until it healed. You were lucky. It healed with only a faint white scar. Though you hated the scar, Annina, however much I told you it was hardly visible.

'You don't see it in the way I do,' you said, and of course you were right.

I thought the cat would have made you more cautious, but it was from then on that you began to go out on your own. You bound waxed thread around the eyelet of a darning-needle, and wore it at your side like a sword. You learned that cats would back off if you screamed at a certain pitch.

Blaise was at college, studying mathematics. When he came home he bent down to me and I kissed his fair prickly cheek with its big pores and splashed freckles and I thought of his sister out there in the jungle with her darning-needle. The bigness of Blaise's hand as he took his cup of coffee. His huge trainers kicked off and lying like mountains on the lino.

Annina, did you love Blaise, your brother? You knew more about him than I ever did. You stayed for hours in his room, listening to tapes with him, watching him study, hearing him talk to his friends. You knew what I didn't know, you heard what only came to me as a drone through the walls. My brother, you always said. 'Do you think my brother will be home soon? Are you making those sandwiches for my brother?'

Your light clear voice and your breath at the curve of my ear. You liked best to talk perched up on my shoulder when I was moving about the house, cooking or tidying, or just sitting with a cup of coffee and an unread newspaper in front of me. And I learned to talk very lightly and quietly too, not whispering because that blurred the sounds too much for your ears. And never shouting, for too much noise made you tremble and curl up on yourself. The only thing that always made you afraid.

Annina, you know and I know that I could go on writing to you for ever, just as I could have listened to you for ever as you tucked your right arm round a curl of my hair and leaned yourself comfortably into the shape of my shoulder and told me things I had never seen and would never have been able to imagine. For we didn't really live in the same world, even though we shared house and home and bed and you shared my body as much as you needed it.

You went away and I have no one else who can talk of you. No one else knew you, no one else misses you or grieves for you. No one else would even believe in you.

You were so sure there were others like you, right from when you were a little girl.

'Have you ever told anybody about me?' you demanded. 'Well then! Nobody does! They all keep it secret, just like you do, for fear of what might happen. We need to find each other. How can I stay here knowing that somewhere in the world there are people like me, people of my own?'

You were like me, Annina. You looked like me. I think even our skins and our hair smelled the same. But that was no good to you, and even though I longed for you to stay more than I had ever longed for anything, I made you a pair of trousers and a jacket from buckskin I got from a child's cowboy and Indian outfit, and I bought thermal silk for your leggings and vests, and you made your own shoes as you had

had to learn to do, for I could never get the stitching small enough, and it bruised your feet.

My son went to college with a trunkful of books and a cake I'd made and a letter a week and a telephone in his hall of residence. He went with a bank account and the name of a doctor and his dental records up to date and his term's fees paid. He went with a pair of National Health glasses for reading and vaccination marks on his arm. He went with both of us waving from the station platform and his father slipping him a fiver to get himself something decent to eat on the train.

It was no good giving Annina money. Where and how could she spend it? My daughter went with a backpack on her back which we'd designed together after hours of thought and cutting the silk into the wrong shapes. Light and tough, that was what she wanted. She went with food and drink and I have to say she went with a great gift for stealing, which I hoped would stand her in good stead when she grew cold and hungry out in the world. She went with her darning-needle sword at her side, and a sleeping-bag filled with the finest down which I'd snipped from duck breast feathers. My daughter went very quickly, slipping through a hole in the fence, following a map of holes and gaps and secrets and hiding-places which she knew and I did not.

I've learned your language, Annina, and now I've no one to speak it with. So I'm still talking to you, wherever you are. It's all right to listen, Annina, for I'm not saying any words that might weaken you. I'm willing you on, Annina, morning and evening. I'll never so much as whisper '*Come home.*'

The Ice Bear

The spicy heat of Stockholm station café knocked her out.
She went limp and drunk. She'd been travelling a long time,
coming home the awkward way through north Germany.
Ferry across the Storebaelt, train, another ferry across from
Helsingør, train across Sweden. Now she was here, still
feeling the bump and rise of travel in the soles of her feet.
She'd worn the same light cotton drawstring trousers all the
way from Yugoslavia, and now she was itchily cold and her
tanned feet looked yellow, not golden any more. There were
three hours to go before the last ferry, the ferry home, sailed
from Stockholm harbour across the Baltic. She could get a
hot bath here, she knew, and wash her hair and strip off her
dirty underwear and change the flimsy trousers for a pair of
jeans.

But she'd been wrong. Things had changed over the
summer she'd been away. They'd closed the bathrooms for
renovations. Only a few showers were working, and as soon
as she'd paid her money and was naked and streaming with
water and shampoo, she'd seen that the floor drain was
blocked in some careful fashion which meant that water had
seeped out into the fresh clothes she'd laid on the tiles outside the shower cubicle, into her towel and her dirty underwear and even into the lining of her canvas boots. Everything
was sodden. She wrung out the towel and wiped the water
slowly and carefully off her shivering body, and then wound

the towel around her head. She had no more clean pants. The dirty ones felt unpleasantly smooth and loose against her skin. She eased herself into her jeans and they gripped her damply at waist and crotch. She'd worn nothing heavier than Indian cotton for weeks, shirts and trousers and wrapover skirts which now lay rolled into faded dirty balls at the bottom of her rucksack.

But at least her leather jacket had stayed dry, hung on the back of the shower-room door. She put it on over her bare breasts and zipped it up to her neck. The springy curls of its sheepskin lining closed over her like home. She was safe again. She started to pick up her strewn dirty possessions. Well, naturally the bath-woman broke into a temper. She was trying to keep these shower-rooms nice for all the passengers, didn't Miss understand. God help us all, she would have thought that anyone would have had the sense to see the drain was blocked and not to use this shower. There was a bell over there, look, with CALL FOR ATTENDANT printed underneath it. Amazing these students, with their university educations, not able to read a simple notice. And it was no good Miss bursting into tears. That didn't help anyone.

The bath-woman bent down from her hips and swabbed the floor with a yellow cloth. She didn't have to do that. She didn't have to present her long-suffering backside to heaven as evidence. She had a perfectly good long-handled mop. But she just knew how bad it would make Miss feel to see the spread of the fat round her back as she bent, and to see the cloth stabbing into the corners of the bathroom, picking up soap scum and long dark hairs and globs of spilled shampoo. The bath-woman knew Ulli's sort. You called them Miss to be civil. Jeans so tight she must've poured herself into them, or else a bit of skirt like a dishcloth showing everything she's got. And then she wonders why she gets herself into trouble.

The café was filling up. Ulli twisted a corner of tissue into a wick to draw up the last of her tears. It was no problem really and anyway she was all the better for crying. She would hang up her wet towel and wash out her bra and pants in the Ladies once she was on the boat. Or why bother? She was nearly home. Three months ago the towel had been striped in dark pink and French navy, but the colours were faded now. She had dried the towel in the air of so many countries. She kept a length of string with her and she could quickly make a line under the luggage racks or across the window of a train compartment. She did not get in anyone's way. She ate garlic sausage when it was offered to her, and she passed her bottles of mineral water and wine from mouth to mouth. She ate heavy yellow Spanish bread, puffs of brioche, black pumper-nickel which reminded her of home, and drank milk cow-warm from a high, green, wet Bavarian pasture where a woman milked her two cows in a shed. *Ice-cold or cow-warm?* the woman asked her. There was a bucket of the morning's milk chilling by the stream.

There were Bodensee apples and split figs from Dubrovnik market. On the Austro-Hungarian border there were baked ears of sweetcorn and tomatoes hanging on shrivelled vines, but no one to sell them. A white dog lolloped through the fields and licked Ulli's feet. A poor skinny creature with yellow teeth spotted brown at the roots, and a healed gash on its right flank. A poor creature but scrabbling and close and companionable. It grinned as Ulli bit into the flesh of one of the tomatoes, as if it wished her well in drawing nourishment from something it could not eat.

At night Ulli rolled up her towel into a pillow and pressed it into the back of her neck as the Japanese do, so that she slept deeply. Very often she did not feel the formal pressure of the customs officer's hand on her shoulder as the train went through some frontier in the middle of the night. She was too deeply asleep to hear voices calling up and down the train asking for papers, or to hear the compartment doors banging open as the frontier guards scanned faces shrunken with sleep. Tanned guards who wore their uniforms easily, boys with good homes near by perhaps, bored but attentive. Sometimes, by the time Ulli woke, not only the customs officials but several other righteous people in the compartment would be calling her through the noise of trains and dreams: MISS, MISS, MISS . . .

So now she had got rid of her tears. She sat in the upstairs café with enough Swedish money to buy herself two coiled buns scented with cardamom, and her own individual pot of coffee. Now a young man came to sit at her table. He glowed in his dark yellow waterproof jacket and over-trousers and his warm, silly cap which must have been knitted by someone who loved him. Or else why would there be so many changes of colour and so many different stitches in one cap? It would have been made by someone who loved him, making work for herself. He took out a book and glanced at her as if he wanted her to register the fact that this was a serious book and that he was reading it. Or perhaps there was more to it. Perhaps he had written it himself, she thought. It had a flat grey cover and thin papery leaves like slivered almonds. It looked as if it came off a small press powered by enthusiasts.

She sat eating her two split buns. She had spread butter on the one half and not on the other, to see which tasted better. Now her body was steamed and hot and fed. She pushed back her damp hair which she'd drawn forward to hide the snaily runnels of tears on her cheeks. Her hair was going into curls. She was just about to unzip her jacket when she remembered that she was wearing nothing underneath.

Before long the young man was talking to her. He too was taking the boat across to Finland. He adhered to a minor Lutheran sect, stricter and purer than the mainstream body of the church, which had gone astray, he told her. It was all very well to run social projects and be involved with down-and-outs and alcoholics, but you got nowhere by ignoring the question of personal salvation. It was Satan who had made us ashamed of the word sin. The young man was going to travel from town to town in northern Finland, on mission work. Every detail had been arranged. He showed her a map, with the towns where he would stay to give the mission marked by green circles. Beside the circles there were the names and addresses of the people who would look after him while he was there, members of the same sect who had been ploughing the ground ready for his seed. Even though he had never met them, they were all his brothers and sisters. This was the first time he had been thought ready to undertake such a mission on his own, without the support of senior and more experienced members. It was a challenge, and a great honour. He had lain awake for several nights thinking of the responsibility placed on his shoulders. Several. That sounded very suitable, Ulli thought. Just the right number of nights to lie awake. Nothing to excess.

But he had to tell Ulli, even though it made him ashamed of himself and he could only say this to her because she was a stranger, that he was torn between love of his wife and love of his mission work. He had just left his wife. He had had to part with her for six weeks. And they had only been married since April. He would show Ulli a photograph. No, it was no trouble, he had one always in his breast pocket.

Ulli did not want to see the photographs. She held her sticky bun out of the way and looked unwillingly at a stiff, bland, white-haired girl on her wedding day. Not much dressed up. It's not the custom with us. In another photograph the same girl was crouching on her skis, with a tiny child wedged between her thighs. The child wore a knitted cap and a snowsuit and had its own small skis. His wife's nephew. His wife loved children and they always liked to be with her. They would ring up and ask if they could come and spend Sunday afternoon with Auntie. She would make sweet cake and tie balloons to the apartment door. She would make little parcels of the cake, in blue and silver paper, and they would have treasure hunts round the apartment to find where she had hidden the parcels. And sometimes she would put in a little verse from the Scriptures with the cake and later on she would sit the children down with her and talk to them about it so that they would understand it.

He showed her another photograph of the nieces and nephews at their summer house up in the north, naked in the sunshine and dappled all over with the patterns of leaves. Their faces gleamed with health. They were blond and well-fed, with straight, even teeth. Animalish, Ulli thought.

'My wife is with her sister now,' the young man said.

But for the moment Ulli had had enough of these holy people with their sweet cake and their shiny metal pails for gathering berries in the forest in autumn and their straight-limbed children murmuring prayers at bedtime. She could see the sisters hunting for mushrooms:

'Come, children, on such a beautiful day let us enjoy what God has given us!'

When they stumbled on a strange blub of fungus lunging out of a fallen branch they would not kick it away in disgust. There was bound to be a lesson in it. They'd take it to the apothecary's to have it checked in the book to see if it was safe to eat.

The young man offered to carry her rucksack to the boat, but she said no. In spite of this he stayed beside her, continuing to talk about the summer house and the forest, and the summer just past, the first summer of his marriage. She would have thought he was drunk if she hadn't known it to be impossible. No, it was just the exaltation of opening out his precious life to a stranger; a stranger who might perhaps profit from it. She was a dry run for his mission. So far he had asked her nothing about herself. Perhaps that came later, or perhaps it didn't matter.

Two station officials strolled by and grinned at the young man. To her it seemed friendly, but the young man was embarrassed and annoyed. Then it gushed out that these same two officials had seen him saying goodbye to his wife not an hour before, which had naturally been a very serious moment for them both. Now they would think badly of him for walking along cheerfully with another girl at his side. They might think that he had arranged to meet the girl and that the kissing and clutching his wife to him had been insincere, one of these games that fool nobody and are not even meant to.

'They were just looking at you. It didn't mean anything,' said Ulli.

Already a slow stain of ideas seemed to be spreading into the gap between the young man and herself. How could she tell him inoffensively that he was not the kind of young man whom girls would wish to meet for brief occasions of sin, after which he could repent luxuriously to his wife? So his

wife had come to see him off. It was necessary to move her
mentally out of the dark forest with leaves falling from the
birch trees and her sister cooking coffee so that they could
talk of mission and chickenpox at the white scrubbed table
while the children played on the lake shore. No, his wife was
on a train streaming its way north through the suburbs of
Stockholm. Perhaps she had a headache. Perhaps she hadn't
managed to get a seat and her fresh bland body was pressed
against that of an engineer who scarcely noticed her because
he was dreaming of his Friday-night sauna and a tall, thick
glass of chilled beer.

Ulli felt scorn for such wives rise in her. Wives who know
somewhere, secretly, that for their warm children to bloom by
the stove and for the coffee to taste as good as it does there
has to be rain beating against the windows and a knife of
wind trying to get in through the flouncy curtains. There has
to be a risk of cuts in social security, and a campaign against
vagrancy. There have to be kids without jobs in too-thin jeans
racing from the launderette to their bedsitters which smell of
damp, in cities where they know no one. There have to be
divorces and children dying of leukaemia and ships going
down and desperate struggles in the darkness.

The young man flipped out his tracts like playing-cards on
the Formica table of the ship's restaurant. In a moment he
was going to look at the menu. There was good Swedish
cooking on this boat, he could tell her that. He had taken off
his waterproofs and bared his intricate jersey of Icelandic
wool. Yes, his wife had knitted it for him. Also the cap.

'I'm going out on deck,' she said.

'Well, that is good, while you are gone I will do my work,'
he replied springily. In just a moment, she thought, he will
put that photograph of his wife down among the tracts. The

ace in his pack. With her there, he will always make the highest score.

Outside the windows Ulli could see people walking around the decks, their clothes blowing lightly against their legs. They laughed as they came round the curve of the ship and the wind caught them. Ulli half-rose from the table, but the young man asked if she would look after his things until he came back from the self-service counter. She watched over his tracts and his good luggage and his waterproofs until he came back with the ship's special, a large all-day breakfast. He put down the tray and spread out his plates, his cup and his cutlery, and then he wiped the tray with a paper napkin and took it back to the collection point. While he was gone, she looked at his food. There were oval slices of sticky black bread, twists of sweet white bread with poppy seeds, sweet-cream butter in a small plastic churn, a fan of sliced Emmentaler and Edam, another of dry pink ham. He had a frosted glass of apple juice, and a smoking pot of coffee.

The young man smiled at her as he sat down and spread another clean napkin in his lap.

He told her that girls like her were always thinking of slimming. It was foolish of them. And the very worst thing was to go without breakfast. Every morning he sat down with his wife to a breakfast like this. No matter how late they had gone to bed, no matter how busy the day ahead – and their days were very busy. Before they went their separate ways they would sit down together and relax over their food and their coffee. His wife always put napkins on the table, and flowers. It was a very special time of the day for them both. Sometimes they'd have important things to tell one another, sometimes they'd just chat.

'It's wonderful,' he said, leaning towards her so she could

see the sheen of butter on the inside of his lips. 'There's nothing I cannot tell to my wife.'

Ulli's mouth was puckering at the sight of so much food. The white, solid, spicy cheese. The thin ham with orange crumbs at the rim.

'I must go out on deck,' she said.

'Yes,' he agreed, 'you look pale.'

She jogged his arm as she squeezed past him into the aisle, but luckily he had not overfilled his coffee-cup. Nothing slopped, nothing was lost.

The ferry was well out of harbour. All around the flat grey Baltic stretched lankly to the horizon. She thought of her last crossing, going west at dawn on a June morning, with the sea alive and transparent all around, lapping the islands as the ship nosed its way between the poles marking the deepwater channel. She had leaned out over the rails to watch the depth change. You could see rocks and white sand with weed rippling across it. They went past island after island, uninhabited, rocky, solitary. Then there had been a bigger island with birch trees and smoke rising from a summer cottage, and a dark-blue rowing-boat tied up at the jetty. They'd passed so close she had heard the water suck at the underside of the jetty. Their wake spun out behind them and the little dark-blue boat went up and down like a rocking-horse.

But now the Baltic had the dark look of late autumn on it. Now the ship throbbed along purposefully, more alive than the empty sea around it. Ulli crisped her hands in her jacket pockets. The wind filtered between the waistband of the jacket and her bare skin. Little prickling slivers of cold. She ought to keep moving. Ahead of her a group of drunken Finns lurched around the deck, arm in arm, the end one of them catching hold of the rail to steady their line. They opened their mouths and bawled out a song which had been on the radio twenty times a day all summer, all over Europe. They were like angry babies with their square mouths and their rumpled cheeks, she thought. They made her tender to them in spite of herself. Small square solid self-respecting men in quilted jackets. Their flesh and hair blending to the same colour as the Baltic. But beneath that blend, a flash of wildness and melancholy, like a knife gliding through snow. She knew them all. They were the men who drank in the bar with her father, though he didn't work with them any longer. Education had moved him on. They were the men who'd found her after-school jobs when she was fourteen. The ones who organized collections for women whose husbands had accidents at work; the ones who planned orgiastic, ritual surprise parties when someone was transferred or retired. She knew how quickly their fierce comradeship of songs and schnapps in the breast pocket could change to fighting drunkenness.

Last winter there'd been an exhibition of drawings from north Sweden in the Town Museum. She'd gone there one freezing afternoon. She'd had three red tulips in a cone of plastic to take on to the house where she was asked for supper, and she couldn't find anywhere to put them down. The cloakroom attendant wouldn't take them. Drawings from north Sweden. Squat dark scrawled people, shovelling earth. Women with muscles like ropes in their necks, wrestling with cattle. All of them lit from underneath with the same light of wild disturbance. A dark skimming line of forest off to the right. The people weren't looking at the clods of earth they turned, or the pigs they tended. Their eyes were pinched and secretive. One man rested on a pitchfork and gazed out to where the dark scribble of trees was stirring in the first north winds of the winter. One woman picked potatoes for the clamp. She had her child pressed against her skirt as she went down the rows of churned earth. Her big hands were wrapped in sacking, but the finger-ends poked out of it, chapped. She had bound her child's feet over and over with more strips of sacking. The child's blunt pale face glimmered against her skirt.

Well then, why aren't I a wife? Ulli asked herself. Why haven't I made sure to have enough money to buy myself an all-day breakfast as of right, and stuff it down in the face of someone who's craving for meat and cheese for once instead of cheap sweet buns? Why don't I feel confident that the facilities of the ship have all been designed with me in mind? And why hasn't anybody told me what they are, those important things I ought to be talking about over a breakfast table set with napkins and roses? How does a young man like that look at me and know without even thinking about it that I'm not wife material?

She turned back. She could still see the young man through the restaurant window. He must have felt her gaze, for without looking up he curled his arms protectively around his plate of ham and cheese. She waved and he looked up and saw her. He looked up and out at her with his pale Lutheran eyes. His big woolly jersey had fluffed up in the heat and steam of the restaurant, like the fur of an animal which scents danger. He had his shoulders hunched and his pale tight curls merged into the wool of the jersey.

Ulli recognized him. He was an ice bear, standing on his own perilous floe of ice. He had bumped and nudged into her and now they were just slipping apart again, so gently that you couldn't tell where the crack had started, how it had parted. The gap wasn't much. Half a metre, then a metre. She could still jump it. But she was better off without the ice bear, she thought. Bears look woolly and white but they'll claw you up for the use of their mate and their young. She'd seen little ice bears gambolling in the wreckage before now, feasting on the bones. The water was sharp and dark with ice. The bear's breath would be meaty and hot, and there would be words like adultery stuck between his teeth.

She'd walk right round the ship. She scooped back her hair and tucked the flap of it into her jacket collar. Now her jeans were dry and warm again, and her blood was beginning to course. The wind from across the sea beat colour into her cheeks as the ferry drummed on across the Baltic. It felt so good to have the weight of her rucksack off her back for once. She knew she could trust the young man to guard it for her as conscientiously as he would guard his own breakfast. Ahead of her, the drunken Finns were blocking the way to the foredeck. They saw her coming and one of them un-hooked his arm from his neighbour's to let her pass. She smiled thanks and he called after her as she went by:

'Miss! Miss!'

She turned and saw he was holding out his bottle of schnapps to her. His friends were smiling him on, smiling their flat curled smiles. A trip for the boys, a day trip or a whole weekend of steady drinking and going wild, away from children and wives. Two swayed together, propping each other. But none of them was out of his head. None of them was fighting drunk yet. They wanted it all to be OK. They wanted her to like their friend, to drink their schnapps. She looked at the man holding out the bottle and saw that to him she was really Miss, in her jacket and jeans just like any of their daughters. Maybe they couldn't understand their daughters either. Maybe their daughters were at university, ill-dressed, no credit to their fathers who had saved up to take them for a meal out at the best restaurant in town. Daughters who spoke scornfully of good jobs, and refused to understand that education was something to make use of.

She could bet the bottle of schnapps that not one of these men had a text of scripture anywhere about him. She took the offered bottle of schnapps, which was wet around the rim with the saliva of the men who had been drinking from it.

'Good health!' she said, and lifted the bottle to her mouth and took one swallow of the dry burning liquid. It went down and lit up the spread of her veins right to her finger-ends. A wave of her newly washed hair curled around the bottle and then the wind flapped it free. She handed back the schnapps to the man who had given it. He ducked his head formally, half in a nod, half in a bow.

'She's not one of those Swedish girls, is she?' grumbled one man on the edge of the group, who was shifting about, restless with all this. But the one who'd offered the drink turned round on him.

'No, the Devil take you, she's not,' he said, in drunken, dignified reproof. 'Are you, Miss? She's one of us. She's on her way home, and glad of it, I bet. She's had enough of those snobs over there with their mouths screwed up like arse-holes, haven't we all?'

No, not a drunken overnighter with the boys. She'd got it all wrong. They were working over in east Sweden, guest-workers of the north, putting in their overtime and keeping their noses clean. And home by ferry two weekends a month. She hoped the ice bear would not ask them to love him for parting from his flowery breakfast table for six weeks.

She thanked the man for the drink. He held out his hand and she took it, and then she stepped away and walked on to the foredeck where a bit of pale autumn sun put a grey shine on the planking. The ferry was going faster now. It creamed away the sea from its sides, and when she put her hand on the side of the funnel it was trembling. She walked on and a hot wall of noise from the engine-room drowned out the men's singing.

The Orang-utans and the Angry Woman

The edge of the zoo lake was furred with picnickers who ate steadily in spite of the off-putting smell of lions. Sheena wished there was a bit of sun for her to sit in. The boys would play for hours by the water. They were hanging over the bridge, dropping lumps of bread into the lake. She had told them not to throw the ham out of their sandwiches, in case of rats. There were three ducks in the murky water, swimming round and round, ignoring the bread pellets as they softened and sank.

She was pouring her second cup of coffee from the flask when the dull peace was shattered. Picnic plates slid about, cardigans twitched, disapproving faces turned, as mean as pennies. Sheena felt a small anticipatory brightening. She liked a bit of life. But a quick glance settled her back on the rustic bench, disappointed. It was just a woman screeching, bent like a bat over her child. A huge woman with a frizz of orange hair on top of her head. Not for this one the hissed threats in the ear, the bribes of sweeties, the furtive slap. She ranted over the child, the flesh of her big upper arms jouncing as she wagged a little pair of knickers under the child's nose. Ridiculous looking nylon things. How could the child's skin breathe?

The woman shoved her little girl this way and that. Fair play to her, Sheena could see stains on the knickers, but it was nothing much for God's sake. What did the woman expect with queues for the toilets a mile long? Lucky that she herself had boys. They had gone behind a tree with no trouble.

The little girl stood without crying. She had a meagre bit of hair plaited up so tight it pulled her eyes sideways. And a white frock on with tats of ribbon hanging off it. She had even put white sandals on the child. What on earth did she expect? How could a child keep herself clean in that lot?

The child lurched, then caught her footing. A man near by half-rose from his picnic seat, looked around for support, settled himself again as if he'd had a bit of cramp. The woman was no fool, Sheena thought. You could not say she was hitting the child. Hard to tell how old the little girl was. One of those queer-faced little souls you see the teacher being kind to. The mother was packed into her sleeveless dress with her great arms chafing the armholes. She had lovely ankles though. A lot of fat people do, thought Sheena. And those neat little baby hands and feet.

Now the woman was tearing at the sash and the fiddly little buttons up the back of the child's dress. The child struggled, twisting away and trying to hold her skirt down over her thighs. Sheena looked round for Jamie and Michael. They were head-down, leaning over the bridge rail, their bare brown legs straining. Michael had got a stick from some-where. They had noticed nothing. The mother got hold of the little girl's joined fists and held them out of the way while she pulled off the dress with her other hand. Now the child hung naked from her mother's grip, in her fancy white socks and sandals. The mother brandished the skinny, cleft little body. Not a mark on her. No, she's no fool, thought Sheena.

'I can never take you anywhere,' said the woman hoarsely, and shoved the child away from her.

The woman searched for a patch of grass which hadn't

been beaten to dust. She spread out the dress. She stroked out the folds so that the fabric would not crease. She rolled the sash and tucked it in at the waist. Her tight permed curls shook a little. She's crying, poor bitch, thought Sheena. Then the woman slid the folded dress into a carrier bag, and laid it on top of her rigid plastic shopper.

Meanwhile the little girl had forgotten her mother and was squatting like a frog, absorbed, teasing a stag beetle. The beetle couldn't get past the barrier of her white sandals. She flicked it with her middle finger so that it fell on its back with its legs waving and its underparts exposed. The man at the next table to Sheena leaned over and said, 'Haven't seen one of those for years.'

'Pardon?'

'Stag beetles. Funny how you don't see them. We used to set up fights with 'em when we were kids.'

The woman had unfolded a red nylon all-in-one splash suit, like the ones the boys used to have. It creaked and rustled unpleasantly as she shook it out. Sheena hadn't known they made them up to such a big size. How old was the kid – six, seven? Without warning, the woman swooped on her daughter from behind and picked her up, holding her under the armpits. The little girl let her body go limp. Face averted, she watched the stag beetle run away. The woman stretched the tight cuffs of the splash suit over the sandals, then crammed the rest of the child's body into the red nylon, and zipped it up to the chin. She took the child's hand, picked up her shopper and set off towards the sea-lions' enclosure, walking fast. The splash suit crackled as the child hurried to keep up.

Sheena had had enough of the zoo. When she called them,

her boys set up a bellow ten times louder than any sound the little girl had made. Reminding them of the ice-cream van just inside the zoo gates, she slotted each child's arms through his rucksack straps, picked up the picnic case and walked off without looking back at her sons. Experience had shown her that this was the way to get them to follow her. At the path fork she glanced back to be sure they had noticed which direction she took. They were scuffling along, heads together, Jamie punching Michael on the upper arm in a way which would have brought roars for sympathy if she'd been there.

Near the entrance Sheena and the boys drew together while Sheena got out her change and told them how much they could spend. They didn't argue. They were good like that, Sheena thought. She watched Michael wait to see what Jamie was going to have, so that he could choose the same. She watched Jamie hanging back from the choice, prolonging the round expectant stare on his brother's face. Just as they were moving towards the turnstile, Michael pulled at Sheena's arm.

'What's all those people there, Mum?'

She saw a row of backs, clustering around a cage. More people were drifting up, curious, joining the little crowd. Jamie was over there at once. He eeled through to the front and then out again, shouting to Sheena and Michael, 'Quick, come over here! The monkey's got a baby!'

Sheena found space at the side of the enclosure. There was a barrier of shrubs in front of the cage-bars, and a big red-lettered DANGER sign. She grasped Michael's hand.

'It's not a monkey, Michael, it's an orang-utan,' she said. 'Mind and stay by me.'

No point telling Jamie. He was already talking to a man with binoculars. He'd come back and tell them all about it.

Yes, there was a baby. It clung to its mother's chest, looking round at the crowd. The mother with her long arms reached through the bar and nipped off a tender tip of green and put it in her mouth. Sheena moved back a step.

The little monkey was learning to climb. First he scrambled all over his mother as she gazed out and away from him. But she must have known where he was all the time, because when he slipped she'd pluck him back to her shoulder without even glancing at him. He muddled himself up in his own limbs and came to a standstill halfway up the cage bars. Smooth and sure, her arm found him. He scuttled across the front of her body into the angle of her chest and her arm. Sheena saw her nipples. Poor creature, fancy having to do it all out here, with everyone staring. She wondered where the baby had been born. Not in the cage, in front of a crowd, surely.

The baby was getting bolder. Sheena could feel the tension in Michael's body as he willed the baby up the bars. It was climbing well now. The little orang-utan rolled out its arm for the next hand-hold, its body a small echo of the mother's. The baby was high now, high above his mother. This time she blinked once, slowly, and did not reach for him. Her baby was spread out across the black bars of the cage-front, small, orange and tender. He stopped and felt for his next grip, and then drew back as if he expected his mother to grasp him. She didn't. She plucked some crimson leaves, and ate them. As the baby went on higher Sheena thought the mother's gaze flicked to him, but she couldn't be sure. Michael called softly, 'Go on baby, go on up! You can do it!'

Other people were taking photos. Smiles pressed in on the cage. By now the baby orang-utan was a good ten feet above his mother and well beyond her reach. But she'd move fast enough if she sensed he was going to fall. Or perhaps she knew he wouldn't fall.

All at once he was coming down, quickly and easily. He looked just like a little monkey. And she'd been thinking of him as a human baby, like her Michael and Jamie when they learned to walk. Now he was clambering over his mother's fur again. Just for a moment she wrapped both her arms around him, folding him close so that all Sheena could see were the tufts of orange fur on top of his head, and his eyes, which looked milky now, like the tired eyes of a baby.

'She'd rip your arm off if you got too close,' someone said.

Already the crowd was breaking up. People closed their camera-cases and grasped buggy handles. Sheena felt Michael lean against her. He ~as getting tired. They'd go home before he started to grizzle and drag at her hand. She'd have liked to say goodbye to the mother, but there were people all around who would hear. And you couldn't get close.

'Say goodbye to the baby, Michael.'

He twisted away, pouting, bored.

'Bye bye monkey.'

Païvi

Really there wasn't room for both of them in the tiny Ladies' lavatory. The door kept butting open with a waft of noise and food smells as yet another impatient woman peered round, and then softened as she caught sight of Païvi doubled over at the sink, her big pregnant stomach bumping the vitreous enamel as she was shaken by wave after wave of sobs. One woman hovered, signalling readiness to help over the back of Païvi's neck, but Ulli shook her head.

'Everything's fine. Just give us a few minutes. She's a bit upset.'

Then Ulli wondered if she'd been right to send the woman away. She wasn't really a friend of Païvi's herself. Certainly not a close friend. She had no useful ideas about what you did to help someone who was due to have her first child next week, and had suddenly dropped her knife in the middle of her creamed potatoes and heaved herself up from the table where she'd been eating dinner with Matti and Ulli and a couple of friends. She'd made for the Ladies so fast that all three men turned to Ulli as if she was a midwife they'd just telephoned.

'You'd better go after her.'

'Perhaps it's starting.'

'She doesn't look too good, Ulli.'

This unanimity of concern hadn't lasted long. Ulli had

glanced back at the table as she opened the lavatory door, and she'd seen them all eating again. Matti, the father of the taut round burden which had forced Païvi to sit two feet back from her dinner, was pouring himself another glass of wine. His fifth, Ulli calculated. Not a good sign. But he was keen on the baby, everyone said. He had two children already, by his first marriage, but he couldn't see much of them any more because his wife had moved up to Rovaniemi to be near her parents – and who the hell wants to spend their weekends in Rovaniemi, taking their kids out for a couple of hours' ten-pin bowling, if they're lucky?

Once Païvi had told Ulli that she had always wanted to have children. When she'd thought of the future she'd always seen herself with a baby. Always, thought Ulli. Païvi was a couple of years younger than her. Certainly no more than twenty-one. But Païvi hadn't got many qualifications at school. Unlike most of Ulli's friends, she wasn't in the middle of a course, or moaning about her tests, or going back to her doctorate after letting it lapse for a couple of years because after all you do need to earn money some time, or perhaps you want to travel, or you're going through a bad patch in your relationship.

Païvi had worked in a travel agency since she left school. The manager was shrewd enough to know that her fair shiny expectant looks had done more to sell fortnights in Rhodes than any amount of exam passes. She had stayed at work up to the last possible minute. They needed the money. Of course Matti had to send his maintenance up to Rovaniemi, and he didn't earn much yet. He was still build-ing up his music business, and although there were lots of exciting projects in the air, and he was having discussions with a big venue in Helsinki which might put on regular gigs, there wasn't much actual money. In fact they really couldn't manage without Païvi's income. Her basic salary wasn't much, of course, but look at all the bonuses she was always getting! And all that just for making herself agreeable behind a desk. Matti wished life could be that easy for everyone.

Ulli couldn't think how Païvi had stuck him for three months, let alone three years. Of course he was very nice-looking, with his slim, dark-featured face and his big eyes which seemed to grow shiny with liking you – at least, for as long as no one else came along. He made it feel as if you were both in something together, up to your necks. Ulli was glad she had a good memory, or else she was pretty sure Matti would have had no trouble convincing her that she'd been to bed with him after some evening of more than usual shininess and suggestiveness.

But none of this was any help to Païvi. Poor Païvi, she looked as if she would retch up the baby if she went on like this. Ulli wished they knew each other better. It had always felt as if Païvi had been completely taken up with being Matti's girlfriend, and then with having this baby, which had drawn her into a circle which was quite different to Ulli's own. Ulli did not want to talk about babies with Païvi. Still less did she want to lay her hand on Païvi's taut and restless stomach, the way some of the men did when they'd had a few drinks.

'God, it's amazing! What does it feel like to you, Païvi?'

About Païvi herself, Ulli knew almost nothing. She was supposed to have absurd ideas about music, touching or embarrassing depending on which way you looked at it, or what kind of mood you were in, if you were Matti. He had pointedly separated his CDs and tapes from hers, in the little flat which had been Païvi's before he moved in. Nobody could make any mistakes about who liked what.

Of course it must be easy to get irritable, jammed together in the tiny flat Païvi had filled with coordinating curtains and chair-covers and pretty wallpaper. She was mad about kids. She had lots of nieces and nephews, and she took one or two of them out every Sunday. She kept a birthday book with all their birthdays written down; she'd even put down their friends' birthdays, and take their friends out too, on trips to the sports hall or to ice hockey. If it was ice hockey, Matti would abandon his principles and go with her. The birthday book had little animals on its cover. Ulli had never seen much of Païvi in the evenings, because she always went out with the girls from work on Friday nights, and then she saw her family, and so on. It gave Matti a bit of freedom.

Païvi straightened up from the wash-basin. She was quite white with big red blotches over her cheeks, and a salty, crushed look round her eyes. Her fair prettiness was snuffed out. Ulli damped a paper towel and passed it to her. Païvi wiped her face with great care, as if she was wiping a dish which she had always liked, even though nobody else much cared for it. Almost all her make-up had come off in crying. Her eyes looked smaller, but still a noticeable blue. She leaned forward and looked at herself in the mirror.

'Oh, I do look a sight. I must put my face on.'

'Are you feeling a bit better?' asked Ulli hesitantly, 'I mean, it might help to talk about it . . .'

Païvi's face in the mirror contracted into a small smile as if she was sharing with herself something complicated and ridiculous which couldn't possibly be shared with other people. She fluffed out her lashes with her mascara wand, drew a perfect line around them with a grey kohl pencil, then smudged the line with a finger. Her eyes, defended once more, found Ulli's in the mirror.

'I just got a bit upset, that's all. Silly, really.'

'It's not silly!' cried Ulli, hot and indignant on Païvi's behalf. 'I mean, if you can't ever show what you feel!'

'But you can't, can you,' said Païvi calmly. 'Not unless you want to put people off. Imagine what Matti would think if he saw me in this state. Thank God we haven't got unisex toilets yet, that's all I can say.'

She blended foundation over her cheekbones and then stroked on blusher. Ulli watched in fascination as she smoothed two more dabs of blusher into the skin above her temples. At once her eyes began to shine as usual.

'I look a wreck,' Païvi commented. 'Well, never mind. My hair's OK, isn't it?'

'It looks marvellous.'

'Yes, everyone told me your hair goes funny when you're pregnant, but it doesn't seem to've, does it?'

'No, it's lovely.'

'I think it falls out afterwards, though. That'll be something to look forward to. Listen, Ulli, can you do me a favour? Get my coat from the doorman for me?'

'Aren't you going to have your dinner?'

'No, I won't. I'll only get upset again. I can feel it. Then Matti'll start drinking . . . you know the way it is. No, I'll go home. I could do with an early night. I might as well get a few before the baby comes.'

'Shall I get him to ring you a taxi?'

'Better not. I'll just slip out. I can pick one up on the centre, easily. And it's not as if it's snowing.'

*

By the time Ulli got back with Païvi's coat, Païvi had packed away her make-up and disposed of the damp towels. She had even wiped the shelf clean. She shrugged herself awkwardly into the coat, and buttoned it over the bulge of her child. The coat did up to the neck, like a little girl's coat. For some reason it made Ulli want to cry herself.

'I bet the doorman thought I'd had one too many,' remarked Païvi.

'No, Lasse was on the door. I told him you weren't well. He was quite worried. You know he likes you.'

Païvi opened the lavatory door, glanced cautiously towards the restaurant tables, and then crossed to the entrance lobby. At the door she turned to Ulli.

'Thanks a million, Ulli. I'm really glad I had you there.'

How can she mean that, thought Ulli. But that small tucked-in smile of Païvi's couldn't possibly be ironic ... could it?

'I'll tell Matti. He'll go home early, I expect.'

'Oh, he doesn't want to bother to do that. I'll be asleep anyway. Don't say anything, Ulli. Just say I wasn't feeling too good, with the baby. Anyway, my Mum's coming down tomorrow.'

'I hope it goes all right, Païvi. You know, in case I don't see you before –'

'Oh, it'll be fine. Just as long as I don't start thinking about it all too much. I'm awful once I get my mind fixed on anything. It'll be fine.'

Ulli walked across the patterned, food-resistant carpet to their table.

'Oh, has she gone home? Well, I expect she was tired.'

'Nothing wrong, was there, Ulli? Good.'

'Have a drink, Ulli. Now, which was your glass?'

'We're thinking of going on to the Blue Vine. D'you fancy it? Matti says they've got a good band playing there tonight.'

The smell of the night to come has settled around their table. They lean forward. Matti'll book the cab. Ulli's dinner has gone cold, but never mind – she can pick up a frankfurter from a kiosk on the way. And then cigarettes. They are nearly out of cigarettes.

'Go on, have another glass. You've hardly had anything.'

And she let go, yielded herself to the smell and the throb of the night to come. Matti was smiling at her, that shiny smile. There were hours to go before morning, hours of night and rushing through the dark in taxis. Who knows where they'd end up, drinking cold beers and ransacking the fridge for sausages? Who wants to be the one who hangs back, who has to go home, who is giving up smoking and only drinks a careful glass and a quarter and won't touch spirits? Because it's night and the night goes on so long.

The Thief

'Come on, Sam. Don't make me late. You wouldn't want to make me late, would you?'

She shakes her head while the hair-dryer frizzes in her ears. She wouldn't want to do anything he didn't want.

'Your hair's gone to fuck.'

She straightens. He reaches out and rubs her hair between finger and thumb.

'Like a bag of crisps,' he says.

'It's always this way until the baby comes. I should never've had that perm.'

He has the jacket, the bag. The bag she'll carry. It is a soft, unnoticeable shopping bag like a thousand others, dark brown striped with tan. In its big heart there ought to be soft drinks, spare nappies, a dummy on a string. But there's nothing. A bag of emptiness, that's what she's got. She'd better fill it quick. It's one of those bags that never wear out no matter what you do to it, no matter how much you come to hate it.

There is no baby in the house. Why no baby? She talks as if there's a baby. Lots of babies. There is a baby inside her, that's for sure. As she stands sideways with the lycra skirt riding up over her bare legs you can see where her belly button has been pushed inside out. That baby's nearly ready to be born.

'When we're done you can go to Children's World,' he promises. He smiles suddenly and she looks at him straight, without expression. In the baby's chest there are nine new-born babygros. She only likes designer ones: Over the Moon, Little Friend, Forever Baby. She wouldn't put a baby of hers into white towelling. She got those special ones for prem babies too. Early Bird. She got six. Shame really to waste them. She's thirty-nine weeks now and as big as a bus, he keeps telling her. Still, she might need them next time.

She needs a Forever Baby duvet to go with the cover. But duvets are big. She'll have to think about it.

'They've got those duvets,' she says. 'Really nice. They go with the sleepsuits, you know the ones I got?'

'You got so much stuff, how the fuck am I supposed to know?' he says, but he's not angry. He likes it really, she knows. He likes things nice, the same as she does.

Her comb sticks and she tugs it gently, not wanting to hurt herself. When she hurts herself the baby shivers and kicks as if he feels the banging too. Who'd hurt a little baby? She knows it's a he. They don't tell you because of these Asians getting rid of the kid if it's a girl but she looked on the scan. Abortion's disgusting. She saw its little thingy on the screen.

She can see the rack of Early Bird mitts and bootees and bodysuits and sleepsuits. Too small for a doll. There was a girl in hospital last time, she'd been in for months. Four pounds eleven ounces her baby was. The midwife was bent down looking in through the side of the box. 'Like a doll,' she kept saying. 'She's just like a little doll.' They were all crowded round, all the nurses and midwives, like it was their baby.

'I don't know what you brought that stuff home for,' he said when she got the Early Bird babygros, 'the way you look it'll be the size of an elephant.'

She gets off the bus. Sun and sea jostle at the end of the

road, but she isn't going down there. She's never liked the sea much, the way it lunges at you. Besides, you can hardly move on the pavement without being shoved around by gangs of foreign kids. It's all right for them. They're on holiday. One long holiday that's been going on ever since she can remember. Some people have got work to do, she tells them. One of them understands and points to her bulge and laughs.

'Work!' he says to his friends. 'Work!'

'Fuck yourself, why don't you?' she says. 'Do someone else a favour.'

She hefts the bag and looks up the square. A double-decker slows for a sleeping policeman and she steps out in front of it, knowing it'll stop. The air brakes hiss and the driver shouts out of the window but she doesn't listen. She's late, not much but enough. No good telling him about the buses though he knows what they're like. It's all right for him on the bike, nicking in and out of the traffic.

He used to take her on the back. All that speed in her hair and the cliffs on their right, the sea waiting for them, She crouched behind him, wrapped to his waist. It didn't matter where they went. Once she looked back and saw rain blowing in like smoke, slicking the road behind them. He was going so fast the rain never caught them.

'Lisa-Marie' she thinks. That's a nice name. Only it's going to be a boy. He won't have her naming it after him.

'Boy or girl?' she said to him but he just shrugged.

'He doesn't mind. He'll love it to bits whatever it is.' She's got the sentence ready in her head but there's no one to say it to. Maybe at the bus-stop on the way back. Someone who doesn't know her.

'What do you want, boy or girl?'

'Oh, we don't mind. He'll love it to bits whatever it is.'

But it doesn't sound right, even coming out of her own mouth in her own head.

She stands window-shopping. This is a snob shop, she never goes in here. She ties her scarf round her head. It looks all right. Lots of people are wearing scarves because of the wind. Then the sunglasses. They look all right too. She makes a tiny face at herself. All right till you look down.

She flows back into the stream. Lots of sales on; well, there's always sales. It doesn't bother her, she likes crowds. Past the doors and the security men standing on either side of them and in through the racks of clothes and the shoppers. She is like a touch-typist. She doesn't have to look at her hands. They do their work while she stares at blouses. Her back knows where to find the closed-circuit telly screen. They think you don't know anything.

Silly cow trying on a jacket, laughing, baby in a pushchair by her, someone else with the baby, both of them watching the baby. Handbag swinging. Move in, past the end of the rail. Her bag swinging. A tiny bump. The woman turns, laughing, sees the big pregnant belly, apologizes.

'Oh – I'm sorry. I'm in your way.'

'*Oh, I'm sorry. I'm in your way.*' Who does she think she is?

She's late. He'll be waiting. When she's finished she can go to Children's World and look at the Forever Baby duvets.

They are round the corner, up the back of Gateway. His hands grope in her bag. He's not good with his hands. He needs her deadpan typist's face and her quick fingers. He doesn't like the way she can do it and he can't. All she's got this time is cash. No cards. She can still see that face laughing, and the baby laughing too. If there'd been a card she could've got the Forever Baby duvet. Doesn't the stupid cow know it's all cards now?

'This is fucking useless,' he says. They are by the supermarket bins. He strips out the cash and throws the rest into the bin. The wind blows the flap of her coat between her legs. He takes the money.

He'll be back later, she knows he will. It is twenty past eleven. From here the sea looks as if it could get her any time it wanted. It's a long way to Children's World but if she has a coffee she could walk up there. She's got the fare home.

'Lisa-Marie,' she says, stirring sugar into the coffee.

'Pardon?' says the woman at the other side of the table.

'Lisa-Marie,' says Sam. 'Do you think it's a nice name?' Suddenly she's hungry, desperate. But the woman grasps her carrier bag handles tight and heaves herself off the plastic bench.

Sam stirs her coffee round and round. The baby'll be Pisces. The way it's lying now it feels as if it's going to come out of her arse.

Last time she was at the clinic the new midwife, the one who hadn't read her notes, bent over Sam and felt her belly, squaring it up between her hands. She said, 'You've got a footballer in here. You'll have your hands full with this one. How big was your first?' Then Anne, the other side of the room, frowned at her and shook her head, a little shake so Sam wouldn't see. They're not supposed to talk about that. Not supposed to talk about what happens after.

Your first. Stupid cow.

'Blood pressure's down a bit. You're doing nicely, Sam.' And Anne gives that smile she thinks covers up what's in her eyes. They think I'm dirt.

'These last weeks are awful, aren't they,' said the new

midwife. 'Bet you can't wait.' And this time Anne walks across to her, pretends to put something on the shelf, elbows the new midwife so she looks up, startled. They think you're thick. Think you don't notice.

Lisa-Marie ought to of kept out of his way. Why did she have to go aggravating him? He couldn't take the noise she made. You couldn't dress her up nice. There was always something. Soon as you washed her face it was mucked up with tears and stuff she'd wiped into her hair. The day he was going to take them to Thorpe Park there was sick all down her new Girlsworld sweat top. Then she started wetting herself though she'd been dry at eighteen months.

'Why can't she use a potty? Other kids use a potty.'

She was like a little animal. She ought to of known better. Then sometimes you'd pull a funny face and she'd still smile at you. Shut my eyes. Click. It's still there, her smile. *Why can't you be a good girl?* And then the noise'd start. Like mewing. You'd go in to her in the morning and she knew she'd been a bad girl. Pull the curtains back. Then the duvet. She's curled up by the wall like she's going to push herself through it. You pull her legs out. Her arms. She won't look at you, she's all scrunched up in herself where you can't find her. Then you say, 'I got your breakfast ready, Lisa-Marie,' and then she looks at you and big shakes start in her and she curls away and you pull her open and then –

The coffee is sweet, just right. The baby thuds into position. With Lisa-Marie the head engaged. That's what they call it. But it doesn't happen a second time. Outside it's raining hard, slashing in squalls across the window. A woman comes in and flumps on to the other side of the table. Big blobs of water skip on to the seat as she fights her way out of her mac. She looks at Sam's belly.

'If they knew what it's like they'd never come out,' she says.

Ullikins

She hasn't found anything for her fat man. She is almost panicking. In the department store mirror her eyes are wide like the eyes of a chased animal. She fingers a dark purple woollen ski-sock on a revolving stand in LADIES SPORTS. Her skin itches at the touch. Who'd wear it? She thinks of white hairy legs marked with the thick welt of the sock. The smell of pine in changing-rooms. Girls bent over, strapping on skis, bright neat curls dangling from their caps. Their upside-down faces laugh and whisper. *Who's going out with Jorma?* Then the first swerve out into the blinding snow. Ulli hooks the socks back over one arm of the stand and gives the stand a twirl.

Sweat prickles her neck. She doesn't like department stores, but at this time of the year you find yourself sucked in to them, hopelessly looking for things you don't want. The store throbs with public heat and with the private heat of hundreds of packed jostling bodies which are jockeying for cheap things to give. Fur caps and jackets make a hive of personal saunas. Ulli has been shopping all afternoon, first buying a plain white quilt for her own bed, then doing her Christmas shopping. The quilt has been boxed for her in Christmas paper and it's tucked behind a desk on the third floor. In her carrier bag she has four stout bayberry candles, a felt waist-coat embroidered with silk for her baby niece, and a sheaf of silk scarves. Light, easy to post, inoffensive. They all have good-quality brand names on them. You can't argue with silk. She's got the whole thing out of the way quite easily this year. All she needs to do now is to slip money, big notes, into a card for her grandmother.

A small crowd has gathered around the ski-sock stand already, attracted by its movement. Black and white zigzagged socks whizz round like weather forecast lightning symbols. Each time the stand slows, somebody pushes it again. But nobody's buying. It's getting late. Little white-haired, ski-suited fuzzballs of children are tearing at their mothers' hands.

'Mummy! Mummy! Get it for me!'

'We'll see, if you're a good girl . . .'

Indulgent smiles have gone rigid, masking irritation. One mother furtively pinches her shrieking kid.

The mothers are candle-white with tiredness, but still automatically turning over yet another tray of those special little Christmas surprises. A tape of Christmas songs, none of them religious, beats overhead. This is the third time Ulli's heard it through since she's been in the store.

> Give me JOY for Christmas
> Give me JOY for Christmas . . .

The store's overhead lighting flickers on and off and a flutey girl's voice comes over the public address system. It's the same pert, lipsticky voice that you hear in all the department stores and railway stations and airport lounges of the world.

'FIVE MINUTES TO CLOSING, LADIES AND GENTLE-MEN! THANK YOU FOR SHOPPING WITH US. WE SHALL REOPEN FOR YOUR CONVENIENCE AT

8.00 a.m. TOMORROW. FIVE MINUTES TO CLOSING,
LADIES AND GENTLEMEN . . .'

A salesgirl in black skirt and white frilly blouse whisks the
covers on to the perfumery counter. The cover flops over a
sign saying WHY NOT PAMPER HER THIS CHRIST-
MAS? Two fat out-of-town women heave themselves
through the store exit just in front of Ulli. Their broad sweating faces gleam as they turn to wedge the doors with their
backsides, and then they hoick their parcels out into the
cold.

'It was worth the trip! We really got some bargains!'

'Yes, and you can always keep those mitts for Antti's birthday. They'll fit him a treat by then.'

But even they haven't bought the purple ski-socks. Ulli
looks back and there they are hanging from the stand, limp.
Then slab after slab of merchandise floats off into darkness
as the store lights go out.

Outside the street rings with sleigh bells, relayed from loud-
speakers stuffed into a Christmas tree at each corner of the
square. Everybody is loaded down with shopping. Her own
bags feel as skimpy and light as air. She ought to have collected the quilt. If she'd been wrestling with that in its big
awkward box, people could have swapped grins of fellow-
feeling with her over the top of their own parcels. But let the
quilt wait, she thinks. It's her own present to herself: a fat
white quilt in a plain white cover that will settle on her bed
like a drift of snow.

There are candles in the windows of the apartments above
the shops. They wink over her head. The warm glittering
apartments signal to one another:

All aboard! Gang-plank up! Seal the windows! We've got dried fish for Christmas Eve and presentation boxes of reindeer's tongue and single white roses in plastic tubes. We've got family photos and grandma's knitting and the kids tucked up in bed with mobiles of snowflakes and story-book quilts. Church at Christmas of course. An hour of boredom to sweeten the dinner! Gang-plank up! All aboard!

In the blocks of apartments door after door bangs shut. If you put your ear to the door panels you'd hear laughter and voices and people protesting: 'No, for heaven's sake! Half that! Are you trying to get me drunk? Just a little one for me!' Visitors. Happy Christmas.

Outside the sky heaves and unrolls another snowfall. The wind lets rip. A faint tickle of it passes through the double-glazed windows. A whine comes up the lift-shaft like the whine of dogs or worse at the long-ago edge of the village. Another packed lift-full of flesh is assumed into warm air smelling of food. Once, long ago, on a lonely night, a poor traveller . . .

In their warm beds children are listening to Christmas stories, the old stories about homeless travellers. It's strange how their parents seem to love homeless people, all at once. 'I don't like you,' the children whisper to one another. '*You're* not my friend.' Their toes curl up under their quilts and they smell the spices drifting from the kitchen. Their sharp little toenails pick at one another's shins.

Ulli remembers her brothers, her three older brothers with their long cold bony feet. They used to tease her at Christmas time, telling her stories about what Father Christmas was going to bring for her, until her head swarmed with greed. They had more money than her and they saved up and hid their savings under their pillows. They let her weigh the thick clumps of coin in her hands. They chose a green phial of perfume for Mother.

WITH LOVE. WITH LOTS OF LOVE. WITH FONDEST
LOVE. WITH ALL OUR LOVE. WITH LOVE FROM US
ALL. TONS OF LOVE. A MILLION KISSES.

Her brothers rolled together, aching and giggling. A green phial of perfume for Mother. Let Ulli hold it. There was a tiny rubber stopper which she had to fidget out with her fingers. Only Ulli's fingers were neat enough. One drop of yellow scent tipped on the inside of her wrist. 'Don't tell! Oh, ULLI! How can you be so stupid?' And she shrank, shamed, to the very edge of the bed, to the cold wall.

She'll never go back. The bunk-beds were sold years ago. Nobody wanted them. Her brothers' children have their own rooms. They need space and privacy, if they are to develop as individuals. Even the baby niece has coordinated lampshade, quilt, valance and puffy curtains. A slow mobile revolves above her head. Ulli's brothers have gone away, to Berlin, to Karelia, to professions and wives. They've left behind dirty toenails and toothpaste going hard in the tube because nobody will ever put the top on. They've left behind pyjamas fished out of the dirty-linen basket to wear for one more night because there aren't any clean ones. They've left behind games in the dark and lying so still you quiver when one of the grown-ups opens the door for a long second and nearly catches you. The grown-up drags on the winking tip of a cigarette while you watch through half-closed eyes. You lie frozen, so still it's a giveaway. But then the huge dark body, Mother or Pappy, backs out of the doorway and the catch clicks and the bedroom ex-plodes in breath and giggles and grappling under the clothes.

'It's about time we moved Ulli out of the boys' room. She's getting a big girl.'

'Oh, Pappy, don't make me. I'll be frightened on my own.'

When she calls her eldest brother on the phone she hears a hiss of silence as he tries to work out how far away she is. Then there's the uneasy flicker of her brother's voice. Sometimes the line goes as dead as a sponge and she knows he's put his hand over the mouthpiece so that he can whisper to his wife:

'It's her!'

'Where's she calling from?'

She hears the wife freeze, stooped over a pile of toys, her soft breasts spilling forward in her angora jersey.

'Is it her?'

'Ullikins, can you speak up? You sound awfully far away . . .'

But Ulli hangs on in silence, letting the line blather and sing to itself. She doesn't speak again. She never says where she is.

The boys used to drag her behind them, light and bumping on their blue sledge. They asked her to choose the colour, and then they painted the sledge themselves. It was the fastest in the neighbourhood. They greased the runners so the sledge swivelled and went wild on hard-packed, late winter snow. She was their little thing. She never cried, no matter how the snow-crust whipped her face. She pressed her lips together tightly and clung on to the sides of the sledge as the boys raced for the top of the run. They passed everyone. They were first.

It was close to dark all day long. In the hollows the snow was blue. Their mother had hung a lantern in the spruce nearest their fence. Its light flared out at them as they swung the sledge round and ran for home. But they turned too sharply and the sledge heeled over on one runner so that it ploughed up a great white wave of snow and half-buried her. Then it righted itself and the boys were charging forward again and she was careering along behind, her body shaking with the bumps, keeping her lips shut. She took in shaky little sips of air and looked down so she wouldn't see them take the next curve. The runners hissed through the snow. She was never frightened, the boys boasted. They told their friends that you could take Ulli anywhere, right down the big runs. She held on. Not a squeak out of her.

All that winter she was the boys' little thing in her navy-blue snowsuit and her scarlet quilted cap. She went down wedged between their knees on the long runs and her head was thrown back against the sharp zip of her brother's parka as the sledge ran over a bump. They skimmed the steep white slopes, and then the boys gave the rope a jerk sideways and they tore off the track, swooping down between trees, whack-ing the sledge in and out of the black trunks as they reared up ahead, again and again until Ulli had to stare down at her own knees so as not to see the snow racing alongside them and the poles rearing up, wicked as horses.

The crust of the snow froze fast. The boys' boots crushed it down with a thick, toasty sound. Once Ulli was walking in the woods, on her own, in the middle of the day. The boys were at school. Mother was sleeping. At the top of the next rise she saw two eyes and the prickling top of a cat's head. Or was it a cat? Its yellow eyes didn't flinch. They stared straight back into hers. Its wild striped coat rippled and she thought of snakes. She could not tell how big it was. The piece of pine fallen beside it might have been a great tree. Pappy had told her about wild cats. Was the rise a long slow sledgers' hill, or just a little lip she could step over without getting snow in the top of her boots? Behind the yellow cat there was more biting yellow sky. Her brothers had told her that there was going to be more snow, a fresh fall. The wind was veering round, they said. The cat's short claws would rip and hurt. She thought of a mouse, mashed up as it ran about trying to keep alive. Did a mouse know how small it was, when it ran about? Did the cat know Ulli was bigger than it was?

Once Pappy had hurt himself because he lost his temper with the boys. There was something in the air all day, crackly, like claws. Mother had been out too long, then she came back and slammed about making dinner. Ulli had her smocked dress on and she was pretty, sitting by Pappy at the dinner table and eating her cold meat in little bites, prinking up her lips. There was screaming round the table but she ate on with her head down, taking smaller and smaller bites, finicking with her knife. Pappy had gone red and raw in the face, crashing after Pekka with his mouth open, bringing his hand down and just missing the arm Pekka threw up to shield his face. Pappy's fist smashed down on the white table with all the force that should have gone into Pekka's face, and Pekka was still screaming with laughter, his hand over his mouth.

Later, she saw Mother and Pappy leaning against the sitting-room mantelpiece, heads together. Mother had one hand on the back of Pappy's hurt hand. She was stirring the joints of his fingers.

'It needs the doctor,' she said.

Pappy humped himself over the mantelpiece and said nothing. And nothing more was ever said. No harsh words. A chaste feel to the house for days. The boys not whistling.

Pekka looking pleased with himself and a little s
had they brought off this time? Mother doing every
people from outside were looking at her. Mother pu
an apron, which she never wore, and baking a loaf of
which griped them all with indigestion. Pappy working late
with a glove of bandage on his right hand. At the office he
said he had hurt it chopping wood for Ulli's grandmother.
About time they got central heating for the old woman!

When the bandages came off she saw Pappy looking at his
own hand with a small proud look, as if he'd been wondering
what on earth it was up to down there in the dark, under the
crust of white bandages which had to be changed twice by a
girl at the dispensary, who was as crisp and fresh as a bandage
herself. Ulli had been expecting Pappy's hand to come out
from under the bandages grey and stinking like the town
flower plots when their ice cover finally broke under the pressure of spring. She watched him sign a cheque. The pen
ticked its way luxuriously along the creamy line of the signature square. His name came out just the same as always. Why
should it be that Pappy's signature was always the same, while
her own veered and wavered from day to day, no matter how
many curlicues she added to it to give it character? You should
never complain of the smell when things unfroze, Pappy had
told them. It was a sign of life.

Ulli stands still in the falling snow outside a block of apartments. This is where she had her first room when she came
to the city. This is where she began to learn to be on her own.
What did she buy for Pappy that first Christmas away?
Gloves. Driving gloves with skinny leather palms. She'd
chosen a plain crimson label. WITH LOTS OF LOVE
FROM YOUR OWN ULLI. A HAPPY CHRISTMAS.

Tons of love.
All the love in the world.
I kiss your hand my darling, before I say goodbye . . .

Then she'd posted the gloves to a friend in Tampere, to send them on from there, so that nobody at home would be able to tell where she was from the postmark.

But never again will she crouch in the right-hand corner of their old blunt-headed Saab, with her eyes fixed on Pappy's profile, diagonally opposite her in the driving seat. When she was very young, she used to think he was always smiling. She saw the lift and tilt of his cheekbones, the hollows under-neath, and she read off the shape as a smile. It was years before she realized that his face was set ahead, impassive and watchful, brooding on traffic or dinner or the Christmas bonus. Her mother used to light cigarettes one after another, and put them between his lips. The boys never came. They couldn't stand being in the car with him.

Years later, the same cheekbones broke through in her own face. For no reason, in shops and queues, in the half-light of cinemas or the glare of sunbathing, she looks happy. She can't help it. Her cheekbones lift and tilt. Her mouth seems to curl up in a secret smile. The planes of her face offer happiness.

'What's the joke?'

'Go on, tell us the joke!'

'Hey, smiler!'

'You look cheerful, sweetheart.'

'Hey, look at her! She's got something to smile about all right!'

'Morning, sunshine!'

'Hello, smiler!'

Ulli shivers. She'd like to run her hands across her face to find out if the smile is still planted there. She has tried hard to uproot it, but after all, you need to be able to smile. And it always comes back, Ulli's little dimple. Perhaps this is why she likes fat men. Not too fat, of course. Not gross. But fleshy men with no deceptive hollows. Men with thick, springy flesh which makes space for her, folds her away, eases her bones. Men who are so heavy on top of her that her breath is crushed to the top of her lungs. Men whose flesh she can wallow in, playing and swimming. Ulli-mouse. Mouse-baby. Ullikins.

Fat men asleep give out heat like furnaces all night. And often they wheeze a little, so that whatever time you wake, however sick and singing your head feels, you know you have company. All night the mattress gives way under their weight and you roll against the elastic warmth of their sides. You know you cannot roll off and away into space. Whatever the bed advertisements say, Ulli knows there is nothing as sleep-giving as the shoulder and breast of a fat man. Ulli's brothers are fit and slim. There is no spaciousness in them. And as for herself, her body looks all dark sharp triangles, from her crotch to the nape of her neck where her heavy plait bisects the twin wings of her shoulder-blades. Her scooped face takes a good photograph from any angle.

Ulli hurries past the restaurant where she ate dinner last night. The fair doorman is taking away a woman's coat. She leans forward like a diver as he peels off the sleeves. Ulli smells meat, but it doesn't make her hungry. She'll go home, take the telephone out of the cupboard, plug it in. She'll drowse on the bed, reading and eating liquorice. Later her fat man will phone her, to let her know he's coming. At eleven-thirty he'll ring her doorbell and shake the snow off his huge overcoat. The cold will have made his nose run. Snow will stand in the close-curled lambskin collar of his overcoat. He'll make one of his bad jokes. He's bound to have a bottle with him, because the fact that she doesn't drink much shocks him, and he hates her prim half-bottles of wine. She doesn't drink enough, and she certainly doesn't eat enough. There isn't a pick of flesh on her. He has no special name for her. He just calls her Ulli.

She'll shut the door and put on Ray Charles. Her room is innocent of Christmas, immune. It smells of the wrinkling winter apples in a bowl by her bed. Without taking off his overcoat he'll sit on the blanket-box by the stove, his thighs spread. He grumbles that she has no comfortable chair. He'll pour himself a drink from his bottle into one of the hand-blown glasses she bought once on a teenage weekend trip to Sweden. They'd visited the glass-blowers in the forest north of Javle, on a soaking-wet late September day. She remembers the little tongs the man used to twist off the end of the glass. Then he snipped it like hot pulled candy.

The glass will mist around her fat man's warm spatulate fingers. He won't move for a while. They never touch straight away, and neither is much of a one for kisses. Only sometimes after sex she'll kiss deep into his thick flesh, as if eating it. He'll sigh hugely as the drink hits him. Later he'll wash and pee with the toilet door shut. They are still careful in such ways. They haven't known each other long.

'Well,' he'll say, 'how's it going?'

A Grand Day

'No, no thank you, I won't. I've my sermon to prepare for tonight.' Laughter. It's a standing joke in the parish that I scribble my sermons on the back of an old missalette, five minutes before Mass. They don't see me sweating for days over a few jokes to put into it. I don't even like jokes in sermons, but you have to have them. People expect it. It doesn't matter how bad the jokes are, though, thank God.

The altar boys are tearing about the car park on skateboards with their baseball caps on back-to-front and their cottas and cassocks stuffed into Tesco bags. The social club ladies are clearing out the parish hall, getting rid of squashed fairy cakes and Twiglets and wiping up pools of lemonade. Bin-bag after bin-bag after bin-bag of it. First Communion over again for another year. I wish the relatives wouldn't give the kids money. I say it every year. A nice book of the saints, perhaps, or a crucifix. Something they can keep. But every year it's the same. As soon as the Mass is over, the kids are in huddles counting out their money.

'How much did you get?'

'My Uncle Jimmy give me a ten-pound note, look at it.'

'My godmother's tight, all she gave me was two pounds and a rosary.'

'I'll swap you the rosary for my holy medal. It's real gold, look.'

'That's not real gold. Don't you know anything?'

A hot day. Great weather, thank God for it. Perfect
weather for taking photographs.

'Will you stand still this minute, Liam!'

'Push her veil back a bit, I can't get her face in.'

'Now let's have them all together. Smile!'

'Don't they look lovely?'

And they do. They do, year after year. The girls in their
white dresses and veils, their white shoes and socks, their little
wreaths of artificial flowers to hold the veils down. The boys
in their white shirts and ties and long dark trousers. Some of
the Italian kids wear miniature tailored suits that cost a fortune, though each year I give the parents the same talk at the
preparation evenings, about how it's not the clothes that
count, and let's keep it simple this year. But they never do. I
have parents on Income Support beggaring themselves to
buy the most expensive First Communion dresses. They'd be
insulted at the idea of anything second-hand.

And they're all smiling into the camera, some of them a bit
shy and others bold as brass, gap-toothed and grinning. Click.
And the next moment they're counting their money again and
spilling lemonade down their dresses and then the day's over.
But they've got the photographs. I banned camcorders after
the Rigby kid shoved her way to the front the year before last
saying she had to be first because her daddy was filming it.
There was very nearly a free fight between the parents of the
kids she'd pushed out of the way and the Rigbys. So it's no
camcorders and no flash photography in church, though it's
hard to enforce. I spotted a grandmother this year filming
from under a spare veil. I could make a joke out of that, I
suppose.

So I'm not going to any of the parties afterwards, though I
must have been asked to a dozen. I go to the First Communion

Breakfast in the Parish Hall, and that's it. It only gives offence to go to one family's party, and not to another's. And I like the quiet when they've all gone.

'It was great, wasn't it, Father?'

'And didn't they look lovely?'

They did.

I wander into the church. It's dark now, and quiet. You can't believe that a couple of hours ago all these pews were full to bursting. Standing at the back, I try to imagine what it's like to look at myself up there at the altar. But I can't imagine it. I am forty-four years old, and that's not an age for looking in mirrors. It seems that you have years and years of being a young priest and then suddenly you look round and you're not young any more. But you aren't old yet, and you begin to get a bit panicky. You remember how sure and settled all those older priests seemed when you were first ordained. And now you are the age they were. Seven years to go before my silver jubilee. Twenty-five years a priest, that's something, isn't it? Of course it is. I'll preach about how it's like marriage. It has its rough places and there are times when you wish you could just walk away. But the bond grows stronger all the time. And they'll look up at me from the pews and they'll be glad I've said it, glad that I'm so sure and settled.

Silver jubilee. And then on through my fifties and sixties, marrying men and women whom I baptized. I've been ten years in the parish, and some of the babies I baptized are coming up for their Confirmations already. It's funny how one or two baptisms stick in your mind out of the whole lot of them. The second Bagenal kid I remember. Andrew. He'd been born fifteen months after the first, and Kitty Bagenal had postnatal depression. They had the baptism the week after she got out of Moorleaze Hospital, and she didn't want to hold the baby. They gave him to me to hold at the party afterwards and there I was holding him for hours it seemed, heavy and warm in my arms, fast asleep. And all the women were saying I had the touch, and saying they'd send theirs up to the presbytery when they cried. He was so heavy in my arms. Warm. He's not turned out so well though, Andrew Bagenal. In with the Child Guidance already.

'Father.'

I turn round, blinking through the dark of the church. I see her like a shadow by one of the pillars. Clare Cullen.

'Is that you, Clare?' I ask, and I hear my own cheery voice die away in the empty church.

'Yes, it's me, Father.'

'Were you at the First Communion? I didn't see you there. It's a grand day, isn't it?'

Grand. I hate that word. But it's the kind of thing I find myself saying all the time.

'Is it?' says Clare. 'I haven't been out much.'

I hold back from pointing out that she must have been out to get here. She doesn't look in the mood to enjoy a joke. She's home from college early. Teacher training is it? I can't remember. Yes, teacher training. She looks very pale.

'I had to come and see you.'

'It's good to see you, Clare. Everything all right at college?'

'No,' she says. She stares at me. Her 'no' swells like a bubble she's blowing, one that will fill the whole church.

'Well, why is that now, Clare? Are you having problems?' I sit on the pew half-turned towards her and smile encouragingly. I have learned all this recently at a counselling course I was sent on. It was supposed to improve our skills in the confessional. Don't judge. Listen. Give the other person space. Think about your body language. I've never felt quite natural since.

'I can't stand it any more,' says Clare, in a low, flat voice.

'What is it you can't stand, Clare?' That was another thing the course told us. Communicate. Use first names. Be there for the other person.

'The way you are,' she says, looking straight into my eyes. I'm so knocked back that I forget all about counselling her.

'What d'you mean?'

'Pretending all the time. Pretending nothing's ever happened. Treating me just like anyone else.'

'Now wait a minute, Clare.' We've had a course on this too. It's not uncommon, they told us. Women get ideas about priests. Fixations. They ring you up all the time. They're forever in and out of the presbytery at late hours, helping organize the Eucharistic Ministers' rota or the Mother Teresa jumble sale. But I have to say I've never been troubled in that way myself.

'Don't tell me to wait a minute,' she spits out, 'I've been waiting three months already.'

'Clare, I think you've got hold of the wrong idea –'

'Oh have I!' she almost shouts. 'Have I! And what about all those letters you've written to me? What about what happened at Easter?'

It's a delusion. A complete delusion. I've heard of these, too. It's all coming clear. She imagines we've had – well, I suppose you would have to call it a relationship. A relationship. I look at her pale face and the soft brown hair round it, always very clean, swinging with the shape of her head. Surely a girl like Clare doesn't need to be having delusions.

'I thought a priest would be different, but men are all the

same!' shouts Clare, and puts her hands over her face. I think she's crying, but she doesn't sob, or go red, or need a handkerchief. She takes away her hands, and then there's a silence, while she picks at the edge of a First Communion poster and glares at me.

I have two alternatives. I could gently counsel Clare into accepting reality, or I could rage back, protesting my innocence and telling her she is mad. But I do neither. A breeze moves in the dark, quiet church. It lifts her hair and lets it fall against the skin of her neck. I find myself smiling. The smile curls round my face like a cat who has come to sleep on a warm hearth. For a long time, it seems, Clare's angry eyes meet mine while my smile continues to grow and settle as if it has come to live with me. The busyness of the morning falls far away, like the clutter swept into the bin-bags. I have no words for what I am feeling. I smile at Clare.

Slowly, her face changes. First she looks puzzled, then little by little a dull pink flush sweeps up over her pale skin, to the edge of her shiny, clean brown hair. Suddenly she looks down and fumbles with the straps of a brown bag she wears slung over one shoulder.

'I'm sorry, Father,' she says.

'What?'

'I'm sorry. I didn't mean –'

She looks quite different. Not flaming with anger. Not even looking me in the eyes any more.

'It was stupid. It was a stupid idea. Oh, I feel so embarrassed.'

And she looks it.

'You made a mistake, that's all,' I say, as gently as I can. My smile has gone.

'No. No, you don't understand. It was a –' she pauses,

and then she gets the word out, 'joke.'

'Joke.'

'Well, not really a joke,' she says hurriedly. 'It was to raise money for charity. We were all sponsored to do our most embarrassing thing. You know Rosie Tyler? She's from the parish. She's got to walk down the High Street wearing a see-through blouse. It's for charity, you see. So I thought my most embarrassing thing would be . . .' she tails off.

'Do they all –' I cough. My voice always gives out on Sundays after the Masses. 'Do they all – know what it was? What you were going to do?'

'Oh no! No!' Her flush is fading. 'Nobody knows, except the student organizer. Otherwise it'd be awful, wouldn't it? We just have to promise that it really is our most embarrassing thing and it's not illegal. Nobody checks up. Well, they couldn't really, could they?'

'How much will you make?' I ask.

'I've been sponsored for fifty-eight pounds,' she says, quite proudly.

'Well, Clare, what do you need? A signed statement saying you've done it?'

'Oh no, nothing like that. They take our word for it. I mean it's not that serious.'

I grin, she grins back. I walk her to the back of the church, talking of anything. How are her studies going? Her parents will be glad to have her home for the summer. No, of course it's all right, Clare. Maybe I'll be putting it in one of my sermons. I could do with some new jokes.

The door opens, letting in a slice of dazzling sun, and she smiles and waves, relieved that I've taken it so well, her clean hair bouncing and shining. I wave back, then I shut the door after her.

It's not that serious. A joke. How could it be anything else? A girl staring at me like that, really looking at me. Her face pale, then flushed red. Wanting something from me. Her clean hair, her warm skin.

'A grand day, Father.'

'Yes, a grand day.'

Family Meetings

Not eat meat! What do you mean, not eat meat? Everybody eats meat, why do you have to be so special? You'll get anaemic. You're pale and pasty enough as it is. Just look at you. And you're always tired. Always complaining when I ask you to do anything. No wonder. How can you expect to have any energy if you don't eat meat? I might have known there'd be some nonsense or another as soon as you went away to college.

Crayfish. What about crayfish? You're not telling me you call crayfish meat! Things with claws that scuttle about at the bottom of the river, you can't call them meat. Meat doesn't scuttle about.

You're going to upset Pappy. You know how he loves to barbecue for you children.

He's missed you, you know.

Besides, just look at the price of all that fresh fruit you're eating! And you gobbled up nearly the whole of that jar of peanut butter.

I just don't understand you any more. What do you come home for if it's just to shut yourself away in your room the whole weekend, eating peanut butter and apples?

But when you smell it cooking on the barbecue, doesn't it make you feel hungry? Just a little bit? Ulli?

'Mummy, I've got a fantastic idea!' says eight-year-old Ulli. 'I'm going to bake a cake for all of us this afternoon, then at seven o'clock I'm going to ring my bicycle bell and it'll be time for the meeting.'

Ulli's mother turns round from the desk where she is adding up figures in a large blue stiff-bound book. She seems to find it difficult to take in the sight of her daughter.

'What? What meeting?'

'I've decided we're going to have a family meeting. We each have a sheet of paper and one of my pencils, my new ones. Then we have to write down all the things we want to talk about in the meeting.'

'What do we want to talk about?' asks her mother. The lazy edge to her voice is very familiar to Ulli, but this time she ignores it. She plunges on.

'It's a meeting about the family. It's about what we like and what we don't like, and how we can improve the family.'

'Is this one of your projects from school? One of Miss Ilmanen's pet ideas?'

'No, it's my idea! I've just thought of it. We'll sit round in a circle. We can have the cake while we're writing the things down.'

'The boys won't do it.'

'It's ice hockey tonight. They don't have to. Just you and me and Pappy?'

'Well. All right. As long as it doesn't take too long. I've got work to do.'

Ulli's mother would like to turn back to her work, but somehow it's hard to do that when her daughter is standing there, glossy with pleasure over some nonsense that Silja really can't understand.

'What kind of cake will you make?' she asks at last.

'A lemon cake. You don't like coffee, and Pappy doesn't like chocolate.'

'For goodness sake don't try to do it without the recipe card, the way you did last time. That sort of thing is only funny once.'

'No, Mummy.'

'Be careful in the kitchen. I don't expect to have to clear things up after you. Good cooks tidy their own mess, you know.'

'Yes, Mummy. You won't know I've even made a cake, I promise. Oh yes you will! You'll smell it baking.'

'You'd better tie your hair back. Here, let me. There you are. Now off you go. I mustn't lose my place in this.'

At one minute to seven, Ulli stands poised with her bicycle bell outside the sitting-room. Her mother is still deep in accounts. Pappy is pouring out drinks for the adults. Ulli races back to the kitchen to fetch herself a glass of juice.

'Silja! Come on now!' shouts Pappy. Ulli wishes he wouldn't. He takes sides every time. Two against one, one against two. Now Mummy won't join in properly.

'Mummy!' she calls, trying to make her voice polite and yet strong enough to carry through to her mother.

'All right, all right. There's no need to shout, Ulli. I'm here,' says Silja. She comes in, blinking because she has only just taken off her glasses. Her fine dark hair is tangled and there is a red dint on her nose where the bridge of her glasses pinches it. Her eyes look very blue, Ulli thinks. They look through and past her family.

'Here I am,' she repeats, smoothing her dark red skirt over her hips.

'You can sit where you like,' says Ulli, taking her mother's hand and towing her into the sitting-room.

Ulli has put out three of the pale beech dining chairs in a

circle in the middle of the best rug. On each chair there is a
sheet of paper, a pencil, and a blue or a green or a violet file
to lean on. In the centre of the circle there is an iced lemon
cake, marked into generous wedges, a jug of water and three
tumblers.

'Choose a colour, Mummy, then you can sit in that chair.'

'Oh, it doesn't matter where I sit,' says Silja.

'It does, it does, Mummy! Choose your favourite colour.
Blue or violet or green.'

'Don't be silly Ulli, you should know my taste by now, I
hope. I like warm colours. Red and yellow and gold.'

'But what about out of these? You've got to choose.'

'Very well then. Blue.'

'Then this is where you sit. Take your piece of paper.'

Pappy, Mummy and Ulli all sit down in their chairs. Ulli
cuts the cake. Pappy takes the large slice she holds out to him,
but Mummy only wants a taste.

'Half that, Ulli!'

Don't try to give her all that, you little idiot! You know she
can't stand it. You know she's got a thing about other people
putting food on her plate. Remember how Pappy used to pick
up her dinner plate with its one potato and little heap of red
cabbage, and tell her she couldn't go on like this, she was
starving herself. And he'd pick up the serving spoon and put
on more potatoes, one, two, three, the biggest, best ones he
could find, and he'd hand her back the plate with the sort of
flourish that men only use when they're taking their wives out
to dinner in company. She never ate the potatoes. After that
she wouldn't even eat the one potato she'd chosen for herself.
She'd start whisking plates around and then the boys would
say they were still starving and so they'd get the potatoes, slid
off her plate.

And I'd sit there with my mouth closed, eating just what I'd been given and no more. No wonder Pekka used to pinch my leg under the table.

Mummy wasn't too thin.

Let's face it, she just didn't like cake. She had never liked cake. Not even cakes made by her dear little daughter who had read far too many children's stories about little girls whose mothers died and left them to take charge of the kitchen and the younger children who learned to love their big sister just as much as their real mother. And of course, to take charge of the father. The father who watched anxiously in case his little daughter grew old before her time. The father who put out a hand to press hers affection-ately when she brought him his evening coffee and shooed the little blonde toddler into the kitchen so that Pappy could have his five minutes with the newspaper. The father who looked up in the long quiet evenings to see his faithful little daughter darning in the big chair opposite which had been her mother's, her fair head drooping under the lamplight . . .

White cakes, oozing buttercream fillings as viscid as oil. The tops dredged with sugar. A stink of vanilla in the kitchen all afternoon.

'Oh no, Mummy, I don't want any. You have it.'

White cakes that set her mother's teeth on edge.

Ulli turns over a sheet of paper which has been lying face-down on the rug. It has a heading in red ink, much decorated with curls and squiggles, rather like the curls and squiggles with which she decorates her cakes. The text is HOW TO IMPROVE THE FAMILY. Seeing it down like that in red and white, Ulli's mother laughs.

'If this is part of a school project, Ulli,' she says, 'I think I'd rather you left it at home.'

'Now, we each take our piece of paper and write down all the things we do like and we don't like, and then how to improve the family.'

'So are you the chairman?' asks Pappy.

'No, Mummy is. I'm the person who collects the papers and reads them – what's that called?'

'The secretary,' says Pappy. 'Then I'll be treasurer.'

'What's that, Pappy?'

'The one who gets the money,' he says with a grim little smile at Silja.

'Or the one who spends it,' she responds.

'It's time to do the writing,' says Ulli. 'And if you want more cake you can have it while we're reading out.'

For a few minutes no one speaks. Silja jots down a few words, casual, bored. Then she tenses over her paper. She writes faster and faster, covering her sheet of file paper with spiky writing. Her smile has gone. Pappy makes headings and writes neatly under each one. Ulli writes steadily and without hesitations, as if she is copying out a composition which she has already done in rough.

'Time to give in the papers,' she says.

The papers are collected and shuffled.

'You'll never be able to read mine,' says Pappy, who is proud of his strong, flowing black handwriting, which looks perfectly uniform but is in fact very hard to read.

'Yes, I will,' says Ulli. 'You'll see in a minute. Now, I'll start with the things we don't like.'

'Give mine back a minute,' says Silja abruptly.

Ulli is about to do so, but Pappy puts out his hand and stops her.

'No, Ulli, read it as it is. After all we're supposed to be honest, aren't we? Isn't that the idea?'

'For Heaven's sake!' sighs Ulli's mother. 'Have it your own way.'

'"THINGS I DON'T LIKE ABOUT THE FAMILY",' reads Ulli. '"Pappy and the boys peeing on the toilet rug. Pappy and the kids following me into my bedroom whenever I go in there to get five minutes' peace, just to ask me whether I'm all right. Not having anywhere private except the bathroom, and after more than ten minutes you start bashing on the door." This must be Mummy's,' adds Ulli. 'Oh, there's another bit. "Ulli sulking all day long and then being Miss Sunshine as soon as Pappy steps in the door." I can't read this last bit.'

'It begins, "Miss Ilmanen",' says Silja.

'Oh, I didn't think it could be that. You can't put Miss Ilmanen in, Mummy. She's not part of the family.'

'Isn't she? You'd think she was from the way you go on about her. Miss Ilmanen says this. Miss Ilmanen doesn't like that. Miss Ilmanen says the evening meal together is the centre of family life. Miss Ilmanen's got a beautiful new wool skirt in blue, my favourite colour. Miss Ilmanen liked my story. I'm sick of the sound of "Miss Ilmanen", if you want to know. She seems a very ordinary young woman to me.'

There is silence while Ulli's fingers scrabble for the next piece of paper.

'You read it, Pappy,' she whispers.

'This is mine,' says Pappy. '"THINGS I WOULD DO TO IMPROVE THE FAMILY.

1 Learn to speak Greek
2 Have plastic surgery
3 Dig for gold under the silver birches

4 Write a best-selling autobiography."'

'But it's all nonsense, Pappy! You haven't done it properly.'

'Yes, it's all nonsense, chicken. That's the only way I can make sense of it.'

Ulli's face is no longer flushed. It is pale, and the little scar over her right eye which she got ice-skating last winter looks dark. She reaches down and picks up her own sheet of paper.

'I'll read mine,' she says. '"THINGS I LIKE ABOUT THE FAMILY: Mummy. Pappy, Jorma, Pekka, Kai. When we do things together. When I do cooking and everybody likes it. Our house. THINGS WHICH WOULD IMPROVE THE FAMILY:

We should not have bad temper or argues.

Pekka should not pick on Kai.

We should be more friendly.

We should have respect for each other."'

'I'm sure she must have done this at school,' says Silja to Pappy. 'Have respect! Where's she got that from?'

'Not from home, that's for sure,' says Pappy, and then there is a stony, glittering silence.

'That's the end of my list,' says Ulli. 'And now we have to discuss everybody's ideas.'

'Is this going to go on all night?' asks Silja. 'I only want to know.'

'I consider all these excellent points!' says Pappy heartily. 'Especially yours, Ulli. We should have respect for one another. We should not have bad temper. We should not have – what was it? Argues? We should all get up at dawn to make each other cups of tea. There might be rather a crowd in the kitchen, but that's by the way. Another drink, Silja?'

'Yes please – well now, Ulli, are you satisfied? Have we done whatever it was that you wanted?'

'It must be about time to ring the bell?' suggests Pappy.

'But we haven't talked about any of it,' begins Ulli. A glance from her mother stops her. 'I'll collect up the papers now,' she says. 'We have to keep them in here.'

Silja and Pappy watch as Ulli clips the sheets together and inserts them in a file on which she has written FAMILY MEETINGS.

'Next time, we'll have the boys, too,' she says. 'They can read the papers from this meeting first, so they know what's happened.'

'Good God!' exclaims Silja. 'You mean there are going to be more of these meetings?'

'I thought we could have one a week,' says Ulli.

'Really, Ulli,' says Pappy, 'don't you think that will be a lot of paperwork?'

'I don't mind!' sings out Ulli. 'And I'm the secretary. Now I say that this meeting is shut.'

'I declare this meeting closed,' Pappy corrects her.

'You can have the rest of the cake now.'

There's a conversation Ulli can't quite remember. It swims like a fish under thick ice. Does she really want to remember it? When did it take place? The last time she went home? No. There was nothing special about that weekend visit, except that it was the last one. Months and months later, when Ulli finally allowed herself to realize that she wasn't going back, its ordinariness became as sharp and final as that of an old photograph found in the drawer of a chest you've just bought in an auction room, which must have belonged to people you can't possibly trace.

It must have been the time before.

Silja, sitting in the kitchen with both hands wrapped round a smoking mug of black coffee. Her face is pinched, but puffy around the eyes. She is not well. It's nothing serious, just diarrhoea, but she can't seem to shake it off. She's lost a couple of kilos since the beginning of the week. Luckily Ulli is at home to look after her.

The house is very quiet. The boys don't come home very often. Pekka is studying in Stockholm. Jorma is in Berlin. He loves it there. Ulli doubts if he will come back. He has a German girlfriend and an incredibly cheap apartment not too far from the Free University. Kai has made a complete balls-up of his future so far, and he is working as a lumber-jack near the Russian border. Far enough from home, thinks Ulli. Not such a balls-up after all, whatever Pappy thinks.

Ulli has heard her mother vomiting last night.

'You weren't being sick yesterday, were you?' she asks. 'Don't you think you ought to go to the doctor?'

Her mother sips the coffee.

'I'm a lot better this morning,' she says, and her yellowish-white face creases into a smile. 'Last night I just wanted to die.'

'Yes, I know, I hate being sick,' agrees Ulli sympathetically.

'No,' says her mother, 'I mean really. I wanted to die.'

'It's the virus,' says Ulli. 'It depresses your system.'

'In that case,' says Ulli's mother, 'I've had this virus for a long time.'

Ulli does not say anything. She sits frozen. She does not want to ask any of the questions which her mother has just invited. For years she has wished that she and Silja were the sort of mother and daughter who would sit in the kitchen over coffee, talking about their lives. Now that it has come, she is terrified.

'I thought I was over all that,' continues Silja. 'It used to be awful sometimes, when you were little. Every day, at some time, morning or evening, I'd think it. "I want to die." It was ridiculous really. I mean, there wasn't any reason. I suppose I must have thought that everybody felt like that. I never told anybody. You didn't have so many articles in magazines then, when you were little. Articles which explained things like that.'

'How old was I?' asks Ulli.

'Oh, I don't know. Six, seven, eight – maybe nine. Then it got better. It started to get better.'

The kitchen is silent. Her mother drinks the coffee. As she does so, a little colour flushes her cheeks. She is starting to look a bit better. She gets up and pulls her dressing-gown around her.

'I'll have a shower and wash my hair,' she says. 'And for goodness sake, Ulli, make yourself a proper breakfast. There's ham in the fridge, and some Edam with caraway seeds, the kind you like.'

'Shall I make you something? Do you feel up to it?'

'No, don't bother. I'll have something later.'

She goes out. The kitchen glitters with sunlight, oozes with the strong fresh light of a summer's morning. Only one more day, thinks Ulli. About twelve waking hours. Nothing can happen in one day. She thinks of the wooden house she shares with four fellow-students. Her bed is waiting for her, rucked-up and unmade. She'll prepare a casserole, layers of potatoes with dill and anchovies. They'll go out to the students' club, and when they leave in the early hours it'll be broad daylight again and they'll walk home along the river with the sun gathering strength and warming their bare arms and legs. They'll have coffee and cakes at the bar on the corner. Not much money left, but it doesn't matter. Ulli realizes that she has been holding her breath.

The sun pours over her legs, which are already brown, which will be dark and perfect before the summer ends.

North Sea Crossing

Carl wakes at six. There are shadows on the ceiling, bright sloppings of sea. Or do you call it a ceiling, when it's a boat? He lies tight under the quilt and watches the room heave. His throat aches, but he knows it's not seasickness.

'You can't be seasick. I've never known it so calm.'

The boat gives a lunge like a selfish sleeper turning over in bed, dragging the quilt with it. His father is buried in the opposite bunk. He never twitches or snores. Once Carl talked about a dream he'd had, and his father said, 'I never dream.' The second his father wakes he starts doing things.

On one elbow, leaning, twisting, Carl watches the water. It's navy, like school uniform, with foam frisking about on top of the slabs of sea. Even through the oblong misted window the sea is much bigger than the boat. He'll get up. He'll go and explore. He'll walk right round the decks and come back knowing more about the boat than his father.

'Hey Dad,' he'll say, 'guess what I saw up on deck!' and then his father's waking face will crease into a smile of approval.

No. Much better to go out, come back, say nothing. Later, maybe, if his father asks, he could say, 'Oh, I thought I'd have a look up on deck.' That way it won't be like running to him saying, 'Look at me! Look what I've been doing.' His father doesn't like that.

'Just do it, Carl. Don't tell the world about it.'

Remember when he'd thought it was a good idea to go out and chop logs. He'd haul in a basket of clean-cut logs, all the same size, enough to keep the fire going for two days. *'Did you do those, Carl?' 'Yes, Dad. Thought we were getting low.' 'Good. Well done.'* But the wood was damp and slippery. When Carl brought down the axe it skidded on the bark and the lump of wood bounced away off the chopping block. And then his father was suddenly there, watching.

'What the hell are you supposed to be doing?'

'I'm chopping some logs, Dad – I just thought –'

'That wood's green. It won't be ready to burn for another year.'

Carl saw his father looking at the mangled wood. 'Next time, ask,' he said.

A small thought wriggles across the ceiling where the sea patterns had played. Why won't his father have central heating like everyone else? Like Mum? No, it has to be a real fire. *'Warm soup swilling round metal pipes – who wants that when they could have a real fire.'* The quilt has slipped off his feet. They're long and bony and they look as if they belong to someone else. The feet Carl used to have don't exist any more. Someone has taken away their firm, compact shape. Now he trips over things and stubs his toes. Last night he hit his big toe so hard against the step to the cabin bathroom that he thought it was broken. He sat on the bunk, nursing it. His toe was red and there was a lump on it that hadn't been there before. The kind of lump a broken bone makes, poking out. If he sucked it . . . He leaned forward, screwed his face round and hoisted up his knee, but he couldn't get his foot in his mouth any more. And it used to be so nice doing that, sending little shivers up the sole of his foot into his spine as he sucked and licked. What if he twisted round a bit more and braced his back against the end of the bunk ... And there he was, knotted, when Dad came back to the cabin. He didn't say anything, just looked while Carl untangled himself like a badly tied shoelace.

There's no more sun on the ceiling. Everything has turned grey, and the sea is quieter, but as close at the window as a bully calling round after school. Its folds look greasy. It's settling down just like Dad said it would. Carl swings his legs and feels for the floor, which thrusts up at his feet like someone pretending to punch you and then pulling back: *'You really thought I was going to hit you, didn't you? You were scared!'*

Anyway, he'll be first washed and dressed. The shower is quite nice, then its trickle of water suddenly burns and makes Carl yelp. But it's all right. Dad can't have heard through the door. Carl comes out, hair slicked back, teeth immaculate. Dad can't stand mossy teeth. Now a thick whiteness is flattening the water. Fog. A second later the boat gives a long scared *Mooo*. 'Fog,' says Carl to himself. 'Fog at sea.' He looks round at the neatness of the cabin. Everything is stacked and folded; even his father is folded away under the quilt, sleeping so well you wouldn't guess he was breathing. 'It's just like being in a ship's cabin,' thinks Carl, delighted. He loves things to be exactly as they should be, no more and no less. But his father has woken up. It wasn't me, it was the foghorn, thinks Carl. He finds he is saying it aloud.

'I know a foghorn when I hear one,' says his father. Then he is out of bed, standing naked at the window. He always sleeps naked. Carl watches the shadow of his father's genitals as he stands there, legs braced, staring knowledgeably into the fog. He reaches round a hand to scratch his buttock. His arms are long. In a minute he'll turn round. Carl looks down. He fusses with the pillow, buffing it up, but as he does so he catches the snake of his father's backward glance.

'What are you doing that for? Can't you leave things alone?' This time his father doesn't say it, but by now the words say themselves anyway, inside Carl's head.

His father wears a watch on his naked body. Now he looks at it.

'They start serving breakfast in quarter of an hour. Stoke up and it'll keep you going. You can eat as much as you want – it's all in the price.'

Carl has read the breakfast list outside the restaurant. Eggs, cheese, ham, bacon, cereals, toast, rolls, jams, marmalade, as many refills of coffee and tea as you want. 'It's a real bargain,' said the woman reading it beside him. 'But only worth it if you eat a big breakfast.' Then she smiled at him. 'I'm sure that won't be a problem.' Why can't they go to the cafeteria? There you can buy a mini box of cornflakes and a giant Coke. In the restaurant he'll have to eat and eat until he feels sick to make it worth the money.

'What's the matter? Feeling queasy?'

There are tufts of hair coming out of his father's belly. Carl doesn't want to have to look at his father's penis, but he can't help it. He just can't look anywhere else. His father's penis is so big and dark and it's the same colour as a bruise. And it stirs. Perhaps it's the movement of the boat.

'No,' says Carl, 'I'm not seasick at all.' But he says it wrong. It comes out as a boast.

'I should bloody well hope not. That sea's as flat as a cow's backside. But visibility's going down,' his father adds critically, professionally, glancing back over his shoulder at the sea as if he owns it.

*

They walk up the staircase to the restaurant. All that is left of the boat's rocking is a long oily sway from side to side. Carl feels tired inside his head. There are plenty of people about, playing video games and slotting coins into snack machines, but nobody talks much. The fog presses down on them all. In the restaurant his father pays for two breakfasts and it costs nearly ten pounds. Carl starts to work out how much breakfast they must eat to justify the ten pounds. As they go past a table a baby is suddenly, silently sick, pumping out a current of red jam and wet wads of bread. Both parents lean forward at once and drop tissues over the vomit. The father takes another tissue and wipes strings of vomit from round the baby's mouth. The baby cries weakly and the father says something, stands, scoops him out of his high-chair and carries him off, held close against his chest.

'Have bacon and eggs,' says Carl's father as Carl puts rice krispies, an orange and an apple on his tray.

'I'm going to come back again,' says Carl quickly. He pours orange juice in a long stream from the dispenser into a half-litre glass.

'You don't need all that,' says his father.

They take seats by the window, looking out at nothing. The noise of the engines is swollen by the fog, as if the boat is sailing inside a box. Carl pours the milk over his rice krispies and raises his spoon to his mouth. His father loads a fork with strips of bacon and cut-up egg. Carl's stomach clenches. His spoon hangs in mid-air, doing nothing. His father stabs the forkful of bacon and egg towards Carl, but at that moment there is a soft 'thuck', a slight, infinitely dangerous noise which silences the restaurant. Its echo is louder than the echo of the huge engines. People look at one another, then quickly away. Carl notices a shiver run down the pale orange curtains. His spoon hangs, his father's fork stays poised in its stab. The boat swings forward like a man gathering himself on a high diving-board. Carl feels his heart tip inside him, a huge tip which will overbalance him and leave him helpless on the floor at his father's feet. Or is it the boat tipping? Someone is putting on the brakes, much too hard. Carl's orange juice glass goes *hop hip hop* along the table, reaches the edge where there is a ridge to stop things sliding, and then falls on to the floor.

'It's all right,' says Carl to himself, 'it doesn't matter. You can go back and have as much as you want once you've paid.'

But his father isn't even looking at the orange juice. He is staring out of the window, listening.

'They've put the engines into reverse,' he says, but not to Carl. A man looks over from the next table. Carl's father is a man people turn to. He always knows what's going on. A small flush of pride warms Carl. 'Into reverse,' he thinks, 'into reverse.' The boat pushes against itself, back-pedalling. Long lumpy shivers run through it, bump bump bump as if it is riding over a cattle-grid.

'Let's get up on deck,' says his father. But there's all this breakfast on the table. Eggs, bacon, rolls, little sealed packets of cheese. His father's coffee has sloped right over the top of his cup and run away in a thin brown stream over the table. Often Carl has thought that his father could pee black pee out of his big bruised penis.

'Carl,' says his father, not angrily. He is right by the boy, standing over the chair where Carl just sits and watches the stream of coffee. He puts his hands on Carl's upper arms. He could easily lift him but he doesn't. His hands tell Carl what he has to do, and Carl rises and leaves the table without giving the breakfast another thought. Everybody else remains at their tables, their eyes following Carl and his father, and at that moment the ship's loudspeaker system begins to honk in a language Carl doesn't understand.

'We've had a collision,' says his father.

Carl looks up at him without speaking.

'It's all right. We'll find out what's happening.'

Behind them people are beginning to struggle up, fumbling for bags and children. There is a lady with baby twins. Carl was watching her last night. Now she staggers as she tucks one twin under her arm and wrestles the second out of his car seat.

'Dad – ' begins Carl, but suddenly they're moving fast, out of the restaurant and nearly at the second staircase which leads up to the deck. People are crowding up the steps. They're not really pushing but Carl thinks that if he stopped they would keep walking over him. But his father is ahead of him and his body is wider than Carl's, making way.

'Hold on to my jacket,' says his father, and Carl gets hold of it with both hands. People dig into him on both sides but he keeps moving, carried up the narrow stairs holding on to his father's jacket. No one would be able to walk over his father. The heavy doors to the deck have been wedged back and they squeeze through, grabbing at the white space beyond.

They are up on deck. An edgy mass of people flows to the rails, but there is nothing to be seen. Only fog, licking right up to the edge of the boat. None of the people round him are speaking English. More sound spurts out of the speakers, but it is twisted up like bad handwriting and Carl can't understand a word.

'It's OK,' says Carl's father. 'We ran down a yacht in the fog. They've put a boat out from the other side.'

The crowd ripples as the news passes over it. It's all right.

No danger to passengers. We've stopped to pick up the crew, that's all. And the hot panicky feeling rolls away into the fog. The lady with her twins is up on deck, and now people are eager to help her. Another lady holds out her hands to take one of the babies, hoists him into her arms and joggles him to make him smile. People find they have still got bits of breakfast in their hands, and those who have picked up life-jackets let them dangle as if they're of no importance at all.

'Run down a yacht,' thinks Carl. 'Splintered to matchwood.' The big ferry thrums and rocks on its own weight.

'How will they find them in the fog?' he asks his father.

'They'll have flares. Let's go to the other side.'

Is the fog clearing? It is whiter than ever, and it hurts Carl's eyes. Maybe that's the sun behind it, trying to break out. There is a sharp smell of sea and oil. Announcements come jerkily, in the same voice they used to announce breakfast and the bingo session last night. It's very cold, and to Carl's amazement quite a few people are going down below, rubbing their arms, making way for one another.

'You first.'

'No, please, after you.'

A man comes up with his camcorder. Its blunt nose butts around in the fog and finds nothing.

His father leans on the rail, looking down. The rail is wet with spray or fog, and it makes a dark bar on his father's jacket. He's looking downward and backward, behind the ship. The speakers sound again.

'They've picked up the dinghy,' says Carl's father.

It all takes so long. Carl is cold and shivering and he can't see much because a wall of adults has crowded to the rail. Suddenly his father says sharply, 'There they are!' He is leaning out over the rail, grasped by two men. A pair of binoculars is handed to him over the heads of the crowd. People shove against Carl from all sides. He can't see anything at all.

'They're bringing the boat alongside,' he hears his father say. 'There's the dinghy.'

His father is the leader. Everyone is asking questions.

'Are they all right?'

'How many are there – can you see?'

And a woman beside him says, 'At least they had time to launch the dinghy. Must've been terrifying. Imagine being hit by this thing.'

Then his father's voice. 'There's two of them. A man and a boy.' Carl hears the charge in his voice. A man and a boy. What sort of boy?

'They're alongside. They'll be bringing them up. Can't see any more from this angle.'

The pressure of the crowd relaxes. Carl wriggles through to his father, who is down from the rail and talking to another Englishman.

' – any more of them?'

' – sailing alone with the boy . . .'

' – bloody awful thing to lose your boat like that –'

Carl stands and watches and listens. A man and a boy, sailing alone in the North Sea. The big ferry like a clumsy cliff bulging out of the fog to sink their boat. He tries to catch his father's eye. He tries a joke. 'Well, at least it wasn't the bow doors! We were lucky.' But his father looks at him.

'*We* weren't in any danger,' he points out coldly.

Not like that other boy. His father's criticism hangs in the air. His father had the binoculars. He'd have seen the boy's face. And the man's, too.

The fog is clearing now. Suddenly, when Carl looks, holes open in it and he can see right along the grey water. It's very calm. He can't help saying, 'It wasn't rough, anyway,' but his father has an answer for that, too.

'That's why it happened. If there'd been a wind it would have blown the fog away. They'd have seen our lights.'

But by lunch-time the whole thing might as well never have happened. They'll be in port in three hours' time. The cafeteria and restaurant are crowded and there is a pub quiz in the Marco Polo bar. Carl has been playing the video games at the bottom of the second staircase. He's done really well on *Rally Rider*. But it's so expensive and there's no one to turn to and say, 'Hey, did you see that? Level fourteen!' His father can't stand video games.

'I might have known you'd be here,' says his father's voice just as Carl gets farther than he has ever got before. 'Come on, we're going to eat.'

They find a table. 'Wait here while I pay for our tickets,' says his father. You have to buy a ticket and then you can eat as much as you want from the buffet. People go past with their trays loaded. There are two empty chairs opposite, and he must keep that one for his father. His father has touched it, indicating that it is his. But then a man puts his hand on Carl's father's chair. He is a big, stooping man with a worried face. Carl blushes and says, 'I'm sorry. My father is sitting there,' but the man just smiles and pulls out the chair, then beckons to someone else. Carl looks. It's a boy, a thin, fair-haired boy about his age. His hair is so pale it's nearly the colour of the salt spilt on the table. The man smiles again at Carl as he sits down, while the boy pushes his way politely down the rows of other people's chairs, and squeezes into his place. The father pats the boy's arm as he sits down. They both have meal tickets but they don't seem to know what to do with them. They talk briefly, seriously, heads close together.

Suddenly, Carl sees that the boy is crying, without sound, pushing big tears away from his eyes with his fingers. His father talks to him all the time in a murmuring, up and down voice, as if he doesn't mind, as if the tears are something he had expected. They're sitting close together anyway, but then the father puts his arm around the boy. Carl ducks his head down and flushes. What if his father sees? What if his father says something in that voice of his that can cut worse than a knife? Even if the boy doesn't understand he'll recognize the tone of voice. And his father is coming back, weaving his way across the room with a full tray in his hand, not holding on to anything because he's got a perfect sense of balance and the sea is as flat as a cow's backside. Carl darts a miserably apologetic smile at his father.

'I'm sorry,' he says, as soon as his father is close enough to hear, 'I couldn't keep your place —'

'No, of course not,' says his father. Carl stares, but can't hear any sarcasm, can't see any cold disgust on his father's face. 'Come on, there are some more seats over here,' continues his father, and leads the way to a nearby table where a family has just got up from its meal. There's rubbish all over the table. Normally his father would hate it, but he doesn't seem to mind.

'Did you talk to them?' he asks Carl, with a little backward nod of his head towards the table Carl has just left.

'No, I – they weren't speaking English.'

'Norwegians,' says his father confidently. 'But I don't suppose they were in the mood for conversation.'

Carl stares at his father, bewildered. Then there is a click in his mind like something loading on to a computer screen.

'Oh,' he breathes, 'it's *them*.'

'Yes, of course. What did you think?'

'I don't know, I –'

'I just hope the ferry company's given them a free lunch, that's all,' says his father.

'But it might not have been – I mean, we don't know whose fault it was,' says Carl.

'Sail takes priority over steam,' says his father, stubbing Carl out. But something's got into Carl. He opens his mouth again.

'That boy,' he says, 'that boy was crying.'

He follows his father's glance at the man, the boy. They are sitting still, close together, weary, their meal tickets crumpled on the table in front of them. Then the man reaches forward and touches, very lightly, his son's hand.

'Reaction,' says Carl's father, 'a perfectly natural reaction once danger's over. They were sailing back from England – managing perfectly well till our bloody ferry went across their bows.'

Across their bows, thinks Carl. What does it mean? He feels his shoulders bow down too, crushed by the phrase, by the cliff of what his father knows and he does not. The engine of his father's scorn churns and cuts into him. Then a small, treacherous thought slips into Carl's mind. He looks across at the father and son at the other table. He's seen something his father hasn't seen. The boy's sliding tears, the father's face bent down to his. That language the man was murmuring. Carl's father speaks a bit of Norwegian, like he speaks a bit of everything. But does he really know what it means, that language the Norwegian father spoke to his son?

A Question of Latitude

It's the twelfth of May. The restaurant garden's open for the first time this season. A waiter goes round with a damp cloth, wiping dust and cobwebs off the white plastic chairs before customers sit down. Farther down, in the more expensive section of the garden where people eat full meals, there are pine chairs and tables, and heavy tablecloths. People here are not yet ready to pay good money for peasant food and boldly checked table cloths. They are only first- or second-generation city-dwellers, and they do not go to a restaurant in order to experience simple, authentic food. They want dishes with rich names echoing the richness of the sauces. They want desserts to make them marvel at the fantastic, throwaway skill of the confectioner. They want release from a sensible diet which follows the advice given in government leaflets and health clinic posters. HEART DISEASE! TOGETHER WE'LL BEAT IT! No, they come to a place like this in order to tell each other: *Go on, be a devil! Spoil yourself! It's not as if we come here every day!*

After all, what on earth's the point of coming out in order to eat something you could just as well make for yourself at home? Celebrations, anniversaries, silver weddings. It's something to have stayed in one piece, never mind married. And the winter's over. An itchy, prickly sense of spring spreads across the pale pinewood and the pale arms, unmarked by tan or freckles, which lie gratefully in the sun's first warmth. The trees move in the light wind, potent with buds which look as sore and protuberant as the breasts of a twelve-year-old girl. They grow up so quickly these days, though their grandmothers can remember being sixteen before they had their first periods. Wasn't there a survey somewhere which showed that Norwegian girls reached the menarche later than anyone else in the world? Isn't that just like the Norwegians! But perhaps the same applies here. It's a question of latitude, perhaps?

The girls at the table have stripped off their jackets and their cotton sweaters. Ulli has rolled her jeans up to her knees, and Birgit has scooped up the two tails of her pink cotton shirt and tied them under her breasts. The fine-grained white skin of her stomach glistens in the sun, and there's a dense pocket of shadow round her navel. There's also a young man at the next table, the son of the couple who are celebrating their silver wedding anniversary. Their only son, it seems, halfway through his military service, his neck tender from shaving and dinted by his stiff collar. His hair kinks at the back, though it's as short as possible, and his ears are scrupulously clean. This is just as well, because you can see straight into them. His ears stick out a little and the sunlight makes them reddish and translucent. There's a fine stubble-fuzz on his upper lip, over his neat and prudent mouth. But his cheeks give him away. He flushes as Birgit catches him staring at her navel. But it's no good: even though he's shy and it makes him ridiculous and he is sure that everyone in the restaurant must have noticed what a fool he's making of himself, he can't help glancing back, just a look, then another look, to where the whole of Birgit's body rises slightly and warmly with each breath, and the gently curving mound of her stomach rises too so that the glisten of the sun shifts slightly, goes back, shifts again . . . The boy gazes, hypnotized, and then he jumps as his mother speaks to him, and blushes again. He drags himself round in his chair so that he can't see Birgit any more, and he picks up his pastry fork to bisect the layers of puff-pastry and ice-cream and glazed apricot which are puddling on his plate. His mother is the only one watching him. Her lips move, unconsciously, as her son swallows his food. He looks up at her, nodding through the mouthfuls of pastry: *It's good, it's really good! And I still love sweet things, just like I always used to . . .*

In a moment she'll push her own plate with its half-eaten pudding over to him. *Go on, if you don't have it it'll just be wasted. And they'll think we didn't enjoy our meal. Go on.*

She's trying to lose weight. The waiters will think that they didn't enjoy the meal, she thinks. She's a woman who always thanks waiters and tells them that everything was delicious, not knowing how they skim the uneaten food into the bins without even glancing at it. It's not really food any more, just stuff which has done its job of being bought and sold. And the pretty waterlily paper napkins go the same way. It's not that expensive here, after all. You get what you pay for, and in this case you haven't paid for linen napkins, or even cotton ones.

She doesn't need to lose weight. When she takes off her pale fussy jacket her arms are solid and smooth. The flesh of her upper arms doesn't wobble, and there is no overhang of fat at the elbow. Her complexion is pale, but clear, the kind of skin which only ever warms to a faint tan. The big solid arms rest calmly against her sides. No watch, no bracelets. She has rings, of course: two on the marriage hand, one on the other, a small opal on her little finger. As she pushes the pudding across to her son the milky opal suddenly spills fire. But she doesn't even glance at it.

'Eat up.'

Ulli and her friends are finished with their omelettes and light beer. Ulli is eating slivers of fennel out of her side-salad. When she breathes in, the air tastes of aniseed. They'll have to spend some more money soon if they want to stay on here, taking up two tables on the sunny deck the restaurant has had built over the river bank. You can look down as if you're a diver choosing your moment to plunge. The river's still swollen with melted ice and water coming off the hills. You would drown in it, but it looks so beautiful with its yellowness and its sucking current masked by the surface dazzle on the water.

They put their remaining money in the centre of the table and there's enough for coffee. Perhaps even a couple of cakes? Ulli counts the money, pushing the coins to one side. Yes, they can manage cakes too. Things are tight at the moment. For some of them the tightness is a pleasurable and precarious game, a game they can rest from in the sudden luxury of a cheque from home or a renegotiated student loan. For others it's not so amusing. Maria has her new bra stolen from the communal laundry-room in the block of flats where she lives. When Ulli calls round to fetch her for a swim later that morning she finds her sodden and convulsive with angry tears, writing out a notice in thick felt-tip: TO THE THIEF WHO HAS ABUSED OUR TRUST AND STOLEN WASHING FROM OUR LAUNDRY-ROOM . . .

Ulli puts her arms round Maria's shoulders as she crouches over her sign, but Maria clenches her shoulder muscles, shrugging Ulli off.

'Leave me alone, Ulli!'

'OK. D'you want me to get some Sellotape or something, to stick it up with?'

'No. I don't! I'll do it my own way! You don't understand any of it – it's different for you.'

'Why's it different for me?'

'Oh, it just is. You're all right, aren't you? You'll always be all right. I don't suppose you're even wearing a bra, are you? You don't need to, anyway. Nothing really affects you, does it? You just smile and put it out of your mind. And you cut people out of your life the same way, when you've finished with them. Oh, I'm not blaming you. It's just the way you are, you can't help it.'

The way you are. Ulli leans back against the wall-hung ironing board. *The way you are. Things are easy for you. I know it's an old-fashioned word, but you don't seem to know what conscience is. Doesn't anything feel wrong to you?* Ulli has heard all this before, but not for years. Not since she left school, not from Maria, not from her friends. Maria's face is patched with crying, and she is twisting a small dry cloth in her hand, one of those cloths you damp and lay over a fine blouse when you're ironing it. Her eyes glow with the joy of telling Ulli, at last, her place in the world. You'll never know all the ways in which you have brought happiness to others, thinks Ulli. Who said that? It must have been years ago. A teacher per-haps, lecturing the class on personal relationships. Well, Ulli has certainly brought Maria happiness. She looks as warm and played out as if she has just had an orgasm. But she's going to spoil it for herself. Already she's regretting her moment of plain speaking, reckoning up the damage it's done.

'I'm sorry, Ulli, I was upset . . .'

'Yes. I know you were. Never mind.'

Ulli has taken up the pen Maria's dropped, and she starts to doodle on the sign. Two little figures: one small, frantic and bra-less, the other running with the bra dangling from her hands and her breasts jouncing, unsupported.

'It'll need a good caption,' Ulli mutters, drawing in more small observant figures peeping around Maria's furious lettering. She'll have to think about what Maria's just said. She can't put it out of her mind. Maria's got such an entirely different way of looking at 'Ulli' that it feels as if she's done something physically painful, like wrestling Ulli's skin until it's inside-out 'Ulli'. Now Ulli's got to look at the inside of her own skin, which is not soft and smooth and glowing with spring colour. It's a bloody dark purple, the reverse of everything she wants to believe about herself. It's strange and frightening, the way her features are gummed on to the bone, when you look from the inside. And her skull's there all the time, with a grin on it which will wait for forty or fifty years to show itself if it has to. When Ulli looked at a skull in the biology lab she thought of it as something which other people have when they die. She runs a finger along her jawbone. You can cry, but your skull's laughing.

She's got to get out of this laundry-room with its smell of fabric conditioner, scorched cloth and sweat. She leaves Maria calmly pinning up her notice, standing back to check that it's straight before she puts on the last piece of Sellotape. In order not to think of Maria and her own skull, Ulli thinks of money. Of course Maria's right. Ulli is broke, but not broke broke. There won't be any cheques coming from her parents, and she's extended her loan as far as it can go, but something good has turned up. She has the promise of a well-paid job from June to September, working for the city's tourist information centre. A brilliant job, really; she won't be stuck in an office all summer long, she'll be out and about, though admittedly out and about in the same places with which she's already familiar to the point of not even seeing them any more. She will be paid a bonus for each foreign language she can offer. She has been reading up on Sibelius, on the shipping trade with Sweden, on the social history of West Finland. There will be a test; guides are expected to be discreetly knowledgeable, to be able to field questions without boring or irritating tourists with displays of unwanted erudition.

Ulli wonders if she will be able to walk across this city and ignore the signs and contours of her own map, her own landscape. Restaurants where she has spent night after night drinking and eating a minimal, required, quantity of food. Street corners where rows have blazed out and she's been left to walk home alone, and other street corners where she has embraced, half-naked, with no matter whom in the middle of a summer night. The towpath in midwinter. The kiosk where she buys liquorice and apple doughnuts and cigarettes, and Vichy water for night visitors. It's a map of lies and secrets. Its contours are the contours of hips and breasts, thighs and genitals. It's a map crumpled with sleep and lack of sleep: sleep in the middle of the day after a long night; white nights when you haven't slept at all and at four in the morning you get up and walk down quiet sunlit streets where all the shadows are in the wrong places. There are things on her map which don't exist. Things she's wanted to believe: who loves whom, who loves Ulli. Who wants to phone her, but has lost her number. Who is tied up in the same sweet bundle of memories with her, no matter where they are. These are things she's mapped her life round for months. Some streets are hot with the first brush of a hand against a hand. There are houses where she's slept for a night or for two nights. Bars which aren't her own bars, where somebody's taken her for breakfast. Changing-rooms where she and Birgit and

Edith have stripped off their clothes and dressed up as house-wives, as cabaret dancers, as teenage disco addicts, as old ladies who like to keep their knees warm. In her map there are clues she hasn't picked up, symbols she's misinterpreted, and words whose meaning she hasn't bothered to check in the dictionary. She remembers a long argument over the word rehabilitation in a bar near the Sibeliusmuseum. Re-hab-il-it-ation. I have rehabilitated myself, I shall rehabilitate myself.

Ulli will rehabilitate herself, in her dark blue uniform with pale blue accents, and a broad ribbon around her plait. She will earn money, too. Ulli will be firmly, discreetly knowledge-able. She will blush, sometimes, to the amusement of business-men who have got daughters of their own back home. It's a gift she's never lost. She'll look like a cross between a nurse and an airline hostess. Moderately sexy, and moderately reassur-ing. She hopes there will be French and German tourists, so that she will be able to put to good use the guide's idioms which she has acquired in these languages. And she'll earn her bonuses.

But it's one thing to show people around your country; even your city. It's another to show them round your life. They will not want to visit the 'old' quarter where Ulli lives. It is not very picturesque; besides, it is cluttered with drunks who may shout at them, and gypsies and old ladies who want to bend their ear for half an hour at a time. And the pollution from the dual carriageway is awful. Ulli will have two weeks' holiday in the middle, that's agreed. Tourist Information does not want its guides to be white-faced, lank-haired and exhaust-ed. They must breathe out the spirit of lakes and forests. Ulli is going to spend a weekend with her friend Edith, who is working on the Helsinki–Tallinn ferries all summer. Ulli can share Edith's cabin – she's cleared it with the ferry company.

Ulli is going to do nothing but go backwards and forwards across the Baltic, lying on Edith's bed and reading Dante's *Inferno*, on which she must write a 10,000 word dissertation in the autumn. Ulli's Italian is terrible, but she is counting on a summer of constant reading. She will not even get off the boat at Tallinn. Edith, in her dark grey uniform, will throw herself down beside Ulli, kicking off the shoes that bind her hot, tender feet, and she'll mispronounce the words as Ulli runs her finger down the text. They'll read the words together, translating them into broken clumps of language, muttering names. Edith will get bored.

Edith's strongly marked lips will be pressed together lightly and dreamily, a sure sign that she's bored stiff. But on the other hand being bored has never bothered Edith. As far as she's concerned her friends have the right to bore her. 'You never know, you may learn something useful,' she says, when people read poems to her in Italian or explain about rebuilding a vintage motor bike from scratch. Besides, Edith can slide back into herself, where no one else comes.

No matter how weak her Italian, Ulli will get to know the *Inferno* like the palm of her hand. Its map, its language, its assumptions. It'll knit up with the flat rocking of the brackish waters of the Baltic, with Edith's breath on her arm, with the soft pressure of Edith's warm side, with the ice at the bottom of the world. Really, Ulli knows this country already, before she even begins to read. She has been there.

She'll read a footnote which asks why Dante chose to expose a man he loved and respected as a sodomite. How did Dante decide to say that this person or that was in his *Inferno*? Why did he select this figure or that for such shame? These are the questions the commentator asks. Ulli will be surprised at the questions. Of course Dante had to say who was in

Hell. After all he had a responsibility as an artist to represent the truth. He had met them there, hadn't he, those murderers and adulterers and liars who seem so familiar somehow, as if they too are living somewhere on the inside of our own skins. How could he have pretended otherwise? Only if he was a liar . . .

Ulli will catch herself thinking this. She'll catch herself spreading out Dante's map of the *Inferno* and studying it like a road-map, clearly marked with short cuts, diversions and all. She'll stop reading and tell Edith, and they'll both laugh at the way Ulli's mind works. Edith will say that she thinks Ulli should have got rid of her medieval imagination by now. All that conditioning! Ulli will have to watch herself if she's going to outwit the inner policeman. God knows she, Edith, has done her best to help Ulli, Edith will say, folding her hands piously. And it's true that the idea of Edith having any sort of inner policeman is far-fetched.

'Let's have a drink. I only get an hour's break now.'

Edith will smile and drink white rum, and close her eyes. But Ulli will read on, tasting Georgian wine, thumbing the inside of Edith's wrist. It's the map of her own country, her native land, her latitude. Perhaps she'll get work as a guide.

Your Body Next to Mine

The water runs softly down her body and into the grass. It is late afternoon but warm, so warm that you don't need to towel yourself after swimming. The water crawls away over your skin like a thousand ladybirds. Josephine lies flat on one of the planked sunbathing decks, her face tucked into the safe personal square her arms have made. Beneath her the wood is worn to a silvery bloom, and there are no splinters. They have all been carried away long ago, in the flesh of other sunbathers.

There is flesh everywhere. Plenty of breasts, proud and substantial and with the slight bluntness at their tips which may be to do with their being Austrian. Or it may not. Josephine doesn't usually see so many breasts, or have so little to think about. Her own white breasts with their bluish veining are tucked inside a black ruched swimsuit and as far as Josephine is concerned they will be staying there. Breasts are all very well when they are so brown, so polished by eyes that they look more like accessories than flesh and blood. But her own in the changing-room mirror are naked as milk.

Next to Josephine a couple squats under a parasol. Each has an airbed. They have inflatable pillows which they wedge under the napes of their necks while they turn their oily faces very slowly side to side under the yellow strokes of the sun. They are in their early sixties, and do not seem to care how much they eat or how big they grow. Since eleven o'clock they have eaten salami in seeded white bread with tiny pickled cucumbers, thin slices of buttercake which they dip into a glass jar of fruit preserves, a basket of white peaches and a flask of coffee. Nothing has been too much trouble. The preserved fruit looms goldenly inside its glass like a bottled foetus in a jar. The husband spears a whole peach, brings it up dripping. They have wine too. They lean off the deck and fish for the bottle where it is wedged upright in boggy water. A good idea, thinks Josephine.

As the day goes on the water gets warmer and warmer, sucking at Josephine's feet like a dog's tonguey kiss whenever she has to clamber down to rinse off sweat and Factor 25 suncream in the lake. The couple watch her attentively as she walks over the boggy ground, back to the sunbathing deck, her body blazing white in the sun. Chaste, black-costumed Josephine looks indecently pale next to all these people clothed in their tans. Her small soft body is meekly downcast, but it makes a number of the stubble-headed fathers of families pause in their tasks of hurling small sons into deep water, or semaphoring at daughters who are paddling inflatable boats too far out into the lake.

There is no wind. Not even a breeze. Josephine turns left and slits her eyes. The white upper slopes of the Wilder Kaiser mountains crinkle. If she moves a finger they will disappear. Up there it has snowed, is snowing, will always snow. The little backwaters of the lake are full of carp. No one fishes. Instead they stand in the middle of wooden bridges, staring down at the peat smog where the fish circle. Bridges, planks and walkways knit together this area devoted to unsoiled nature. Josephine has seen hundreds of carp and has stopped looking at them. Once she watched a parachutist land on firmer ground on the other side of the birch trees, and once a water-snake swam deep under a family of ducks. No one else seemed to see it. She pictures herself brushing the dusky bellies of carp, her feet twined on weed. As she swims perhaps she will see the narrow head of a snake part the waters and sail alongside her, a long rippling V growing behind it.

'*Bitte.*'

The woman next-door – yes, it's just as if they are each in their own suburban garden – offers Josephine a small silver fork on which a segment of pineapple drips syrup. She nods encouragement. *Go on, have some! It won't kill you! Skinny as you are.*

Won't it? Josephine can't bear, simply can't bear anybody feeding her. Once a really quite nice man tried to drop grapes into her mouth one by one. He must have seen it on a film. At first she protested laughingly. She'd never found it easy to get angry when she was naked. But he kept on, his big mouth grinning above her. Suddenly she saw all his teeth. One of the grapes burst on the pillow. She was going to roll on it if she wasn't careful.

'No,' she said, trying to keep her tone light, 'no, no, I really don't want any.' But as soon as she opened her mouth he crammed in a grape and tried to follow it with his tongue. Gagging, she sprang bolt upright, clutched the sheet round her breasts and spat out 'Don't you ever listen, idiot!' along with the crushed grape. Next thing he was hopping about the bedroom floor, stamping into his underpants with his back to her. No, Josephine can't bear being fed.

The pineapple smells of alcohol. The little silver fork winks in Josephine's face. '*Bitte schön.* You don't eat anything,' says the woman. Her husband grins approvingly, his lips rolling back from a wide ring of teeth.

'Oh. *Nein. Nein danke*,' says Josephine. Is that right? But the woman waves the little silver fork encouragingly, as if she were trying to catch a fish.

'Oh, OK,' says Josephine. It will be too awkward, stuck bang next to these two for the rest of the day, perhaps for days to come. She's noticed how everybody seeks out the same square feet of planking each morning. A rejected pineapple piece might grow to the size of the Wilder Kaiser mountains by the end of the week. 'I mean, *danke*.'

She smiles, opens her lips, her teeth, nibbles the cube of succulent pineapple in between them until it is hidden and then shades her smiling eyes as if the late low sun over the water is dazzling them. She turns sideways, reaching for her sunglasses, and in the second when her face is averted from the couple she spits the cube into her other hand. Sunglasses on, hand folded at her side, she turns back to the woman. This time there is a cherry on the spear of the fork. The smile is broader now, complicit with the secret greed in Josephine's slender body. The pantomime of refusal and acceptance must be gone through again. But this time Josephine is wearing her sunglasses, so she has to reach for something else. A quick sniff, the back of a hand to her nose, the fumbling for a tissue. She has palmed the cherry.

The woman is as relentless as a fruit machine. Does she know what Josephine is doing? No, that's not possible. She beams at her husband with transparent glee as she feeds the foreign woman with cherry, apricot, grape, kiwi slice. The gritty slither of kiwi nearly defeats Josephine, but a pretended adjustment of her swimsuit strap takes care of it.

Suddenly there is no more fruit. Smiling, benevolent, the couple retreat behind their magazines. They have done their best with Josephine. Some people need to learn to enjoy themselves.

Josephine lies still, fruit sludge sticky in her left hand which dangles loosely, at ease, along the silvery-pale boarding. A shadow stops above her.

'You took your time,' she says.

'The agency was shut till ten-thirty. If I hadn't stayed we might not have got reservations. You were all right, weren't you?'

But he scans her quickly. The possibility of her not being all right is another shadow, deeper than his own.

'I quite liked the walk here,' says Josephine.

'Did you?' he asks eagerly, and looks around at the view as if to see what she has seen. Lake, mountains, the white combing wake of water-skiers, the woman who has just climbed out of the lake with a baby twin on each hip. Now she steps with magisterial purpose towards the shower. She presses the cold-water button with her elbow. He notices that she doesn't shut her eyes although long needles of shower-water are running all over her face. She hunkers down, one twin clamped between her knees, the other in her hands. Her costume is exactly the same colour as her tan. Another fifty yards, distance, and she would look naked.

Josephine lies face down on the boards, her white legs trailing. The light is turning yellow. Edward looks along the spongy, impossibly green grass of the lakeside and sees what looks like quite a nice tea place. This is the best time of day, when you come out after the last swim. You shower, and then comb back your wet hair, squinting at yourself in a tiny crazed mirror. A pee feels like the final act of cleansing. Your sweatshirt is soft and grateful on your arms, which have begun to feel a chill. And when you walk out your feet slap on warm pine boards. But he's only just got here. He hasn't swum once this holiday. Josephine has her chin on her hands and is looking at him. 'Your whole day wasted,' she says.

'Not wasted. I did see something of Innsbruck. And I found a nice place for lunch, we ought to go there. You'd love Innsbruck.'

But they won't, she knows. She tries to imagine it. Walk from the hotel to the station. Train. People in their compartment. Traffic, crowds. An escalator at the very least, possibly a lift.

'All the same, a whole day out of your holiday,' murmurs Josephine.

It's late. A file of laden homegoers crosses the little wooden bridge. Children sleep against their fathers' necks, dazed with sun and water. Birches drip thicker and thicker shadow. And the couple next to her – next to them – have got out another flask. This time it is tea. The husband pours rum into his tea from a tiny bottle.

'*Tee mit Citron oder mit Rhum?*' he asks his wife, as courteously as a waiter in an expensive hotel. Yes, there are lemon wedges too, wrapped in a plastic bag. But the wife nods towards the rum. After all it's a holiday, why not? Edward smiles. He would have the rum too. He remembers when Josephine started to drink hot water with a slice of lemon in it as soon as she woke up. It set his teeth on edge. He was always up first and he'd brought her a cup of tea and toast with cherry jam, every morning since he could remember. Always cherry jam. But suddenly she didn't want it any more.

'They haven't stopped eating since they've been here,' says Josephine rather loudly. Edward frowns. 'Don't be silly, they don't understand. Why don't you lie down? It's perfect now. Not too hot.'

But she'll have been lying in the full glare of the sun all day, he knows. She would never hire a parasol, or choose a deck under the birches. He has to rub sunblock on to the parts of her body which she can't reach, the back of her thighs, her shoulders. But when he's not there she manages. Josephine is as supple as a contortionist. He lies down carefully. His canvas deck shoes were new this morning, but they have a dirty rim of peat round them now. 'The lake flooded,' says Josephine. 'It was three feet deep here last month. They've had a terrible season.'

She always knows things like that, although he never sees her talking to anyone. But people always want to talk to her. Look at the woman next to them, giving her fruit, trying to make friends.

Josephine's been quietly working away since he got here and by now she's hollowed out a little grave for the spat-out fruit in the bog by her hand. Her fingers are filthy. He watches them pat smooth the jelly-quaking ground where she has buried the pineapple and cherry and peach. She wriggles her fingers in the grass to clean them and then smiles up at him.

'You managed then,' he says.

'Oh yes.'

Without me hangs in the air. He sees himself sweating round Innsbruck, noticing things for Josephine, worrying about her.

'Lie down,' she says, pulling him with her sullied fingers. His new Chinos creak as he lowers himself to lie beside her. There is the strong scent of her hair, and the vanilla smell of her shoulders.

'You'll have to be careful you don't burn,' he says. 'This sun is hot.'

'I won't burn.' She reaches out and hooks one of his

fingers with hers. This is how she likes to touch him. She smiles a deliberately childish smile.

The couple next door start to clear up. They pack everything very carefully into a white and blue insulated bag, and then the wife lumbers to her feet while the husband flattens their hissing airbeds and telescopes the parasol. She watches him with a smile. A nice smile. The smile is for Edward too, as if he were part of it, the packing and unpacking and eating and clearing away. But the smile misses Josephine whose eyes are shut and whose fine-grained skin gleams over the delicate structure of her shoulder-blades.

There is a bit of sausage left. The woman pauses in her packing. It is not worth wrapping in the waxed paper and taking home. But good food – a crime to waste it. She has never been able to bear wasting food, from a child. She looks at Edward, sees him looking back. Her experienced eyes take him in. A businessman in holiday clothes, solidly built with a roll of flesh around the stomach. His suits would hide it, but those Chinos don't give a man a chance. They are clothes for kids with empty bodies. She glances at Josephine's long, narrow back, sheathed in black ruching. Josephine's thighs are as white as paper. Unhealthy. The woman smiles at Edward, removes two slices of rye bread from another waxed packet, and carefully sandwiches the sausage between them.

'*Bitte*,' she says to Edward, proffering it. He takes it, smiles, nods his thanks. Josephine has turned slightly so that her cheek is pressed against the satiny surface of the sunbathing deck. She is watching him out of one half-shut eye, her fastidious face taut. Edward opens his mouth wide. He bites.

Smell of Horses

The thick yellow light of a mid-July afternoon wobbles through the bathroom fanlight. It spreads and breaks into golden lozenges on the bare skin of the six women in the bathroom.

This room hasn't always been a bathroom. The big, square, late-nineteenth-century house belongs to Birgit's great-aunt, who went into a Lutheran Home in the city a couple of years ago, and said she'd leave the house to Birgit in her will. But Birgit insists to all her friends that she doesn't want it. Whatever happens, she won't live in it. Ulli doesn't know whether she says this to her aunt when she goes to visit her in her packed hot room in the Home, or whether she only says it to the women friends she asks out there for summer weekends. Birgit is twenty-four now, a student of philosophy, a city girl who has cut her long white hair short and crisp and close to her scalp. This little Swedish-speaking town on the west coast, with its neat-framed church and its little alleys which duck between the houses, is as familiar and stale to Birgit as the smell of her own past. She has chopped off this past as she has chopped off her hair. It's the past of a good girl with long plaits who studied hard and was her aunt's favourite. A girl who sat reading by the stove while autumn winds funnelled and whined past the house.

The whorled pattern of the stove tiles has burnt into Birgit's finger-ends through hours of boredom, hours of

159

listening to stories and being trotted out to the old ladies who visited for coffee and cakes and stayed all afternoon without ever taking off their hats. When Birgit touches people, she cannot help leaving that print on them, the print of long, intimate bourgeois gatherings where the pastries are never quite as light as they were in the old days. But Birgit is twenty-four now, a student of philosophy and as hopeful as an exorcist.

The light is liquid. You could smear it like golden slime. There are six women in one bathroom. The bathroom used to be a bedroom. There's still a mahogany picture-rail, a soft, flowered carpet and a chaise-longue covered in moss-green velvet, picked and rubbed. The bath stands a metre or so out from the wall, on its own green-bronze claw feet. The big taps splay out water so fast that the bath fills in less than a minute.

The bath is full of water. It came rushing out of the taps colourless, but now it sways and waits and it's green, the colour of the new growth on a spruce. Ulli has been walking down by the shore, on the swampy, reedy, straggling outskirts of town where there are two peeling white houses like eyes staring off into nowhere. Her legs are scratched by the reeds and streaked with mud. She stands by the basin and flannels them down, pretending to herself that she is flannelling the legs of a horse. She is pleased with her legs. They are firm with exercise, and they have a tan which is neither too dark nor peeling. She had them waxed in a salon in the city a couple of weeks ago, so they are smooth and shiny. Mud fans out in the washbasin, and she pulls the plug, leaving a water-mark of grime. Now she's clean enough to go in the bath.

Of the six women, four are naked. Birgit is shaving her underarm hair with a clumsy steel razor she's found in the cabinet. She's put in a new blade out of a packet wrapped in waxed paper, and there you are – the thing may look Victorian, but it still works. Sirkka refuses to look at it. She says it sets her teeth on edge. She cannot bear to see the bloody, light-red nicks which it makes on Birgit's white armpit. Then there is Ulli, now moving away from the wash-basin, stepping out of her khaki shorts and pulling her halter-neck top over her head. The top is butter-yellow, and the nicest thing she has to wear this summer. There are Sirkka, and Birgit's cousin Edith. Sirkka is perched on the broad sill of the bath, hunched forward, her heavy round breasts dipping and swinging between her gesturing arms as she talks to Edith, who is seated on the big old-fashioned lavatory. This lavatory has a vast bowl of crazed ancient enamel, and a wide dark mahogany seat which matches the picture-rail and the shelf above the bath, and strains your thighs when you sit down on it.

Edith's thighs are wide apart, and she holds the front of the lavatory seat like the pommel of a saddle. This is her way of relaxing, she says. If she tenses one set of muscles, another will loosen. Edith has just announced to the roomful of women that she is dying for a crap and she hopes nobody minds. Nobody answers specifically, but there is a general murmur which suggests that nobody does. Besides, any crap which comes out of Edith's firm slender body will surely be as inoffensive as a child's.

Two other young women, childhood friends of Birgit, are setting out cards for Patience on the flowery carpet-meadow. They are dressed in cut-off jeans and shirts. They really have been out riding, and they smell strongly of the sweat of the horses, and of their own sunbaked hair. It's Ulli's turn for the bath first, and then they'll go in.

Ulli kicks her pants under the bath. She doesn't wear a bra

with this particular sun top, but because she's been sunbathing in her bikini for weeks she can't get rid of that bra-and-
pants look, which is printed on her in white. She doesn't like
it. By the end of each summer she aims to be smooth and
bare, all of a piece, all of one colour. Birgit has told her that
it's fine to sunbathe naked on her great-aunt's back porch,
which is secluded and ringed with lilac and silver birch, and
so Ulli plans to take out a blanket and sleep there in the late
afternoon sun, once she has had her bath. One of the other
women will rub her with sun oil. There's a bookcase full of
late Victorian and early Edwardian Swedish novels which Ulli
has never read. Or perhaps she'll drift through *People in a
Summer Night* yet again . . . ?

They'll eat late, about nine. Nothing fancy, just a cold table,
with pickled herring and smoked meat and potato salad with
dill. Edith can make stars and tulips out of tomatoes. Sirkka
swears by the natural yoghurt which she makes fresh every
day. It's sharp and acid, but all the women feel sure it's doing
them good. Sirkka's had problems with thrush for years, but
not a moment's trouble since she started making her own
yoghurt. She eats it neat, without so much as a pucker of the
lips, but the others crush in raspberries and bilberries and
whortleberries, and then swirl clear honey over the fruit.

They'll eat and drink until their heads buzz and then they'll
stagger about saving the big moths that fly in through the
open windows to char themselves on the lamps. Ulli will write
her diary in enormous sloping letters which Birgit can read
over her shoulder. A little later Edith will sing and Sirkka will
hum along in her husky, cracked little voice which would
sound terrible on its own but weaves in quite sweetly with
Edith's. Ulli will play easy pieces on the walnut piano which
Birgit still hasn't bothered to get tuned, because she's not

going to live here, she's never going to live here. This is just summer life, she says. She likes to share it with her friends, with Ulli, with Sirkka and Edith, with the little girls she ran with and screamed with and fell in love with when she was a child. But Birgit doesn't see that each filament of summer life is binding her in its own way, pinning her down as she sprawls so carelessly and nakedly in the grass of the backyard, or in the green swaying bathwater, or on the chaise-longue as she half-dries herself and then lets the remaining droplets evaporate slowly from the long blank canvas of her skin.

Ulli slides down in the water. She has hooked her long plait over the back of the bath, and it tugs the hairs at the nape of her neck. A sharp sensation, neither pleasant nor unpleasant, marries itself to the lukewarm lipping of the water at her breasts. One afternoon Birgit stood behind Ulli the whole time she was having her bath, and held Ulli's plait free of the water. There was no tug, no sharpness, no discomfort. But Ulli isn't going to let her do it again. It isn't fair to Birgit. It's not as if, at the end of each long slow cooling evening, Ulli is the one who goes over to Birgit and hauls her to her feet, losing balance a little so that both women stumble and sway and have to put their arms around each other to get a grip on each other's weight. It isn't as if Ulli does that for Birgit, or tends her when she drinks too much and cries and then says the next day that it's nothing, it's just the stress of her course. There are too many tests in Philosophy, Birgit says.

Ulli loves to stroke Birgit's soft hedgehoggy head, newly barbered: barbarous, to the spirit of her great-aunt who has overseen so many night plaitings.

Ulli shifts her body from side to side in the bath and the water rocks up one side, then up the other. She can see right up the greenish inside of the wide-throated taps, which are not very well cleaned under the régime of Birgit and her friends. This makes Ulli think of looking up the insides of bodies. Kids, best friends, frenziedly devoted, picking one another's noses, rolling earwax and swallowing it.

She raises one leg out of the water. The skin turns silver in a bar of afternoon sun. Ulli balances on one elbow and runs a finger down the inside of one calf, wiping off water and sheen. Now Sirkka climbs up on the edge of the bath to open the fanlight and let out the smell of Edith's crap, which after all smells much the same as any other human adult's. As she stretches up Ulli receives a dizzying vision of her long full-fleshed tensed leg going away and away into the light like a ladder to heaven. The muscles in Sirkka's buttocks flex and gleam as she undoes the catch and shoves the sticking, corky window-frame open. Edith turns from wiping her backside and smiles up as at a benediction. Ulli closes her eyes.

Now she cannot tell where she is. The water is at exactly the temperature of her blood. She lowers her head until her ears are underwater and hears the bath boom and thud like her own circulation. She lets her body slop from side to side. She pretends she is a seal clambering the steeply sloping con- crete sides of its zoo pool, bruising its wet black nose. She slips back into the bath, burying herself in the water. Only the twang of her plait at the nape of her neck keeps her the right way up. Then she rolls right over and crouches on all fours and ducks her face under the water and opens her eyes so she can see shifting squares of sunlight rove over white enamel. Her eyes sting and she comes up.

The two friends-from-childhood have finished their Pa- tience and are looking over the edge of the bath and wonder- ing aloud how long Ulli is going to be playing about in there? Isn't she going to wash herself and come out?

'In a minute,' says Ulli.

They pass her a bar of Birgit's expensive transparent soap and Ulli soaps her belly and her pubic hair then sinks down under water again. Dabs of soap foam float off across the water surface. Ulli's eyes are level with the water and she watches the foam drift away from her like summer clouds moving springily towards a horizon: clouds which never turn to rain. She hooks her toes round the taps and then shoves off so the whole soaked arc of her body shivers through the bathwater one last time, and a fat wave flops over the back of the bath and on to flowered carpet and cut-off jeans and warm biscuity knees.

She can smell horses.

Cliffs

There's a file of murky cuttings in the local newspaper archives which shows the village as it once was. From the yellow and black fog of dots you can pick out dumpy cottages which have long since slithered into the North Sea. There's a woman standing beside one of them, stout and grim-faced. She'd lived on the edge of a cliff with warnings in her ears for so long that when it came, that lugubrious parting rumble of earth from water, she had her black-clad Bible to hand and simply began to read the text she had already chosen.

But times change. People who live in Marring now hold as hard to the notion that they are entitled to long life and fruitful retirement as Mary Anne Walters did to the turning leaves of her Bible while salt water washed it to pulp. They pay their council tax and expect the services of geologists, climatologists, sea-defence experts and Dutch marine engineers. And all for one village, mutter their inland neighbours. One little village whose inhabitants wouldn't give the snot out of their noses for anyone not born and bred in the place. The vans roll in with their cargo of young chaps barking into mobile phones, come to study the latest crack in the cliff, the latest gape of subsidence in the wall of the old graveyard. The graveyard itself has long since disappeared.

They drive home before dark. The long banks of sea fog that wait just beyond the horizon roll in most nights, like old friends warming themselves at a fireside. As it blankets the houses of Marring the fog brings with it the smells of things the sea has long since swallowed. The bitter elder and ivy smell of the lane beyond the graveyard where lovers met to fight free of their virginity. The tang of autumn leaves heaped up by Charlie Hellus' broom, where nothing but seaweed now swans with the tide. And the smell of Mary Anne Walters' sheepshead broth. But no outsider ever smells any of these, for they come after dark when business is over.

The cliffs at Marring are the colour of the red in those red-and-green rubbers which erase both pencil and ink. They fall straight down to the water below, like a child's picture of sea and cliffs, but their sheerness has nothing to do with innocence. They are wily twisted things in their hearts, those cliffs, though they look as solid as a pound of old-fashioned mints on pension day. They know how to lull those who watch them.

Look at the cliffs up close. There are slithers of water all down their face, like rats wriggling out of holes. And the sheer raw red breaks up into a thousand particles of shifting, shuddering sandstone and mud. But no one looks this close. No one can. They walk along the spit of shore which the sea has left to them, and they throw balls for dogs whose yapping climbs the cliffs, penetrates them, eases their fabric apart by another thousandth of an inch. And the sea twitches at the foot of the cliffs, all its fur rolled into points by the bright offshore wind.

Twenty years ago one of those hippies came. He set up in the house closest the cliffs. Gone now. Tom Marl's house. He got called Tom, too, the hippy. Not that it was his name. Was it in an Austin he come in, one of those eleven hundreds? No. A

Mini. Surely you ent forget the flowers on it. Tidy car. But he let it rust. He'd no call for cars. Said he'd done with travelling.

It was the day after Tom Marl's house went down. Course he knew it was coming. The hippy, Tom Two. After he put all his worldly goods by the ice-cream sign outside the Stores he went back to watch it. Nothing to watch. Only the gape of the door and behind it a space where Tom Marl's house was due to drop.

It was a bright morning and the sea was beaten up in foam, jumping about like it knew what was coming to it. You could see the gulls flying through the space where Tom Marl's windows was. And Tom Two says, 'I'll climb that cliff.'

He did too. With half his house hanging off it. He went up to the lip of it and felt about delicate, like it was the lip of a girl. He'd took his boots off. Then he twisted his hands in a tuft of grass and his bare feet squirmed into the first of those watery holes all down the cliff face. Like walking in cheese. Yes. But there were twenty gathered down on the shore by then and they say he danced down. They watched him. Half his house hung up above and the rest of it the sea was picking apart like a woman at a jumble sale. Some bits he lost his footing and slid, but each time the cliff caught him. Looked like it didn't want to throw him off. He was raw red when he got down, and he ducked right into the water to wash himself.

He came back the way we did. Along the shore and up the steppings. The rest of his house hung on. How many months was it? Then we had a storm and it walked into the sea. Never seen the cliff so red as it was the next morning, where it'd been sliced off. You'd a thought it was still shivering. Like when a butcher cuts the meat through so clean it doesn't know it's felt the knife.

Tom Two was staring at it. 'Missing your house?' some fool asks him.

'My climb's gone,' says Tom Two, staring at it. He missed that climb he'd done more'n he missed the house. And he was staring and working out how he'd climb that new cliff that was as wet and shiny as redcurrant jelly.

He did. He let it dry out and four days later he was on it. He stuck halfway down but he thought his way off of the ledge while we watched him. Couldn't get up so it was down or nothing. There was babble about holding out a blanket for him, like fluffing up cotton wool under a man falling from an aeroplane. He came down. No foothold or hand-hold so he dug himself into the cliff where it was softest, making up to it so it'd let him pass over it. Never seen such a thing. It was getting misty and the sun dropped as we stood, little red ball hopping down the sky till it sunk in the water. What if it gets dark, they said. What if he can't see? Darker it was the better he liked it. There's things you can't do in daylight.

Each time it broke he climbed it. Oh, he was living in Charlie Rend's place now. He'd a gone on for years climbing and digging Charlie Rend's vegetable patch, except for Tracey Ellerton's piano. When I say Tracey's, it was from her gran. That girl'd never've had the gumption to get herself a piano. And there she was moaning in the Stores cos Ellerton's was next to go. They'd had the surveyor round to tell them. Not that they needed telling, they could see the cracks. But Tracey wouldn't see it. She'd rung up every piano-moving firm in the book to get em to shift it but nobody'd touch the job. And then round she goes asking the lads if they'd move it for her. But if you've ever heard the earth grumbling when it wants to move you'll know the sound there was around Ellerton's, and none of them'd go near the place. Nice piano, mind. A baby grand. Tracey couldn't play a note.

Tom Two was in the stores. 'I'll shift it for you, Tracey,' he says. Well, there's nothing between him and Tracey Ellerton. She's a bit taken back, but he smiles and says, 'Don't you worry. I'll get that piano out of the house for you.' So she says right.

He gets ropes and canvas webbing, the sort they use to pull a cow out of a ditch. The house is moaning by now. It knows what's coming to it. 'Don't do it, Tom,' says Tracey's mum. She knows her Tracey can't play a note. But Tom just tells her to get a hold of the rope and sling it round her trailer hook. They've the van backed up to Ellerton's, as close as it's safe.

There was the sea below, flat as a map. Its work was done. You could see the curtains shudder in Ellerton's windows, though there wasn't a breath of wind. And then Tom went in. He made nothing of it, stepped through the door as if he lived there.

Must've been his weight. We heard a sound like yawning.

'She's going,' someone said. Tracey was crying. Then Tom came to the window. He pushed up the sash, called out, 'I've tied the ropes. Get ready to pull,' and then he give us the thumbs up. Then the front of the house sagged like a man falling asleep upright. The kitchen window frame dropped straight out on to the grass. We saw the door-frame tear up from the step. The bricks jiggled and the chimney-pot starts to topple, but it was still a house. And then for a moment we saw them all at once, the way you see your life before drowning. Tom Two, the television, Tracey's magazines, the live bricks and the skin of plaster over them, the fridge, the bedclothes and that blessed piano all dancing round in the same space like they'd got to know one another for the first time.

And then the house reared up and was gone. It was a long time later we heard the sound of falling.

When they were gone we all went down to look at the cliff. It was a big slab come off that time and there she was in her new face, bright and shiny as a copper penny. You'd think she'd miss the feel of Tom Two's climbing feet, but she can't show it. 'There's things you can do in the daylight,' Tom Two used to say, 'and there's things you do best by night.' And who's to see them, when everyone's tucked in their houses and the fog's up? That's when Tom Two comes. You'll hear him whistle like a man does when he's glad to go to his work. And she's waiting for him. She's missed the feel of his climbing feet, and his hands too, the way he stretches them out and feels for the soft places in her.

Girls on Ice

Ulli has studied the brackish waters of the Baltic in high-school science. She remembers field trips when she had to sample and test sea water before reading up on experiments which reported the leaching of DDT from the shores of our great neighbour into the tissues of Baltic herring. Our great neighbour. That was what they'd called the Soviet Union then. Ironic, derisive. That was the way to survive. There are no national borders as far as pollution is concerned, their teacher had emphasized. They should arm themselves with information. It was their future.

But there were so many campaigns. Campaigns against heart disease. Campaigns to solve the energy crisis. Campaigns against alcoholism. They'd been bored kids in caps with ear-flaps, trawling the water to see how many life-forms it supported, looking sideways at each other, grinning and giggling. The environment was less fashionable then. She recalls the very words, held in the glassy tissue of boredom like flies in amber. The relatively shallow, brackish waters of the Baltic freeze easily. Leaving aside, as someone had whispered, the fact that it's fucking freezing anyway.

Girls by the Sea

There's a good title for a painting. Or it could be a chapter heading for a novel perhaps? But not a good title for a poem. Girls by the sea. No, it definitely wouldn't work for a poem.

You would begin to think of something sad, something elegiac, something long-gone. Long-gone good times.

Girls on Ice

No better. Trying to be ambiguous. Trying too hard. Can anybody trust a story which starts by shoring itself up with double meanings? Perhaps it's only by not having a title at all that you can hold on to the itch of the moment.

It's very cold. A yellow snow-laden wind is just veering round from north to north-east. Ulli and Edith are walking south-west over the ice, out to sea, and now the wind's blowing directly behind them, butting them along, wrapping their long coats around their thighs and knees so it's hard to walk straight. Edith clutches her fur cap down with both hands. She wears a very soft pair of fur-lined leather gloves which once belonged to her grandmother. The surface of the leather is finely crazed with age, but the gloves are supple and warm. Edith can remember holding her grandmother's hand and stroking the fur cuffs of the gloves. Now her own fingers have replaced her grandmother's.

Ulli's family does not have such things to hand on. Gloves made of the finest leather that could be bought. Made to last. And a bargain, really, if you look at it the right way: once acquired, they last through generations, just like money does.

Ulli is all in brilliant Inca wools: a cap of layered colours, a long scarf which she's crossed over her chest and knotted at her back, and a pair of mittens in ochre and terracotta. Her coat is a heavy secondhand wool greatcoat from a church used-goods store. She has dragged it in at the waist with a wide leather belt, and its skirts flap around her ankles. She likes the contrast between her own narrow waist and the wide swirls of heavy cloth.

Both girls wear laced leather boots with strong crêpe soles which grip well on the ice. The boots are a neat matt black, and they fit tightly around the ankles. They look rather like Edwardian skating-boots, the kind with holes in the bottom into which you screw the blades. The girls share a detestation for parkas in muddy primaries, for built-up snow-boots and thermal caps with ear-flaps, for mittens with strings which run through the armholes, for padded vests and all-in-one zip-up suits in scarlet or turquoise. In fact they avoid all sensible, practical outdoor clothing of the type listed as suitable for high-school cross-country ski trips. Edith will spend hours washing lace in weak tea until it acquires just the right patina of age. Ulli has spent a fortune on silk thermal underwear so that she need not mummify herself in heavy jumpers all through the winter.

Girls on Ice

Here and there the ice surface is churned by tyres. Away to their right a yellow Saab is nosing its way out, squat as a pig truffling for fish. As far as they can see the Baltic has just stopped still as if a traffic policeman has put his hand up.

'It depends on what you mean by love,' says Edith, skirting a Sitka spruce someone has dragged out here with the idea of lighting a bonfire on the ice. But the fire must have fizzled out, or perhaps someone else put a stop to it. One branch of the spruce is charred, that's all, and the ice is puckered up where the fire has touched it.

Ulli pretends not to hear what Edith has said. She wishes she'd never brought up the subject. They've had this conversation so many times. Is Jussi getting hurt, is Edith responsible for this, is there anything anybody can do about it, ought

Edith to pull out of the relationship even if it makes Jussi unhappier than ever in the short term . . . ?

And whatever anybody says it doesn't make the slightest difference to Edith. That's just not the way she thinks. From her point of view, everything's fine. Jussi's having a good time. He must be, or else why would he stay with Edith? After all Jussi's free to do as he pleases, isn't he? Nobody is making him stay. Certainly not Edith. People should relax more, Edith thinks. Why are they always talking about relationships? Either you are having a good time with somebody, or you aren't. If you aren't, talking about it doesn't help. And besides, Jussi is so moody these days. No fun to be with at all.

And Ulli can't help feeling that there's a great deal in what Edith says, even though it does make some of her friends so indignant that they stop discussing relationships with Edith and start shouting instead. There's certainly something lacking in Edith, they say to one another afterwards.

Edith is a fashion student. She's set up her loom in the house where she lives with four other students and she weaves marvellously rough bright cloth out of which she cuts jackets and coats. One boutique is taking her clothes already, though their mark-up is scandalous, Edith says. In a year or two, when she's built up her stock, Edith's going to open a shop of her own, in partnership with two other final-year students. There's no doubt that Edith's going to make it. This winter she's trying out a technique she calls scrap-weaving, and the room where she sleeps is covered with pieces of experimental cloth. She's making up small, close-fitting jackets, like skating jackets. There's a woman in England who breeds a particular type of long-haired sheep, and Edith's got some wool samples from her; Jacobs, the sheep are called. Edith is making drawings of brief, smooth, long-haired skirts.

Girls in Short Skirts

They could walk on the ice in their short skirts, with thick tights and legwarmers and boots. Why not? They'd lose that nipped-in Russian look, that lovely balance of torso and leg, but they'd gain something nice. The sense of striding out.

Men Looking at their Legs

Yes, there'd be that of course. Does Ulli mind? Does Edith mind? Their legs are bold in dark green thick-ribbed tights and diamond-patterned Inca leg-warmers. Their legs are not anybody's easy meat. They have no desire to wear glossy nylon and to strip off their frozen skin along with their tights.

It's nearly too cold to think. They go on squeaking over the ice, not wanting to turn back and walk into the wind. When they look back, the wind slashes at their eyelids until they brim with tears. A curd of snot freezes from Ulli's nostrils to her lips. The shore is so far away. How far they've come, much farther than they meant. The town is just a little clutch of houses, humped round by low hills. Ulli feels as if she's swimming miles out. She'd like to lie back and scull the water with her hands. She'd like to float on her back as close as possible to the surface of the water and to the warm sun. She must block out of her mind the dark depths of the water heaving underneath her. When she looks back to shore she feels a shiver of fear, emptiness and weakness, as if her blood is pouring out of her.

Girls on Ice

The only ones out here now. The yellow Saab has crawled back to its heated garage, and the kids who were practising ice hockey and shrieking across the bay to one another have all gone back home to drink hot chocolate and make up their team lists. Because soon it's going to be dark. Already the horizon is folding in all around them. Already the reed banks have gone, and the spruce plantation behind the reeds. Blink, and the dusk thickens. Two soft round lights come on where the town is, and then there are more and more, coming on in warm rooms, as distant and inaccessible as the lights of a liner passing close inshore with a long moo from its foghorn. Blink, and you'll miss the way home.

'We'd better go back,' says Edith.

They turn, and the wind bites into them, glazing each particle of exposed flesh with frozen tears. Ulli's greatcoat flaps open and a knife of wind slides up the inside of her thighs. She trips, and barges into Edith. They just can't walk fast enough. The wind is shoving them offshore, like a flat hand saying BACK, BACK! But they are glad of its noise as it whines and buffets past their ears. They know for sure that they are too far out. The sound of the wind will hide from them what they are afraid to hear: the slow creak and unzipping of the ice. No good telling them now that the ice is solid from here to Ahvennanmaa. Out here you have to believe in ghosts and in ice spirits and broad-backed monsters breaking the surface with their snouts.

The girls link arms. This way it's easier to walk against the wind. They have to keep their heads down.

'Don't keep staring at your boots,' shouts Ulli, 'it'll send you to sleep!'

God, that is the last thing she needs. A sleeping Edith, keeled over on the ice, confident that everything's going to be all right.

It depends on what you mean by love.

*

A cuff of wind throws the girls sideways. Now there are particles of ice in it. The air's blurring. And surely it isn't quite so cold? The temperature's going up quickly, towards freezing-point.

'I think it's going to snow,' says Edith.

'You don't need to shout about it!' says Ulli. She doesn't want to give the weather any more ideas than it seems to have already. Now she remembers someone telling her that there's a current around here. It curves past the headland and then sweeps in close to shore. You want to watch that you don't get caught. But she didn't take much notice at the time. Who was it told her? It must have been some time last summer. They must have been going swimming, or perhaps Birgit had planned to take the boat out? They hadn't taken any notice. Birgit knew the coast like the back of her hand.

Now Ulli looks up and sees the snow coming from the north-east. The snow rushes towards them like the great filtering mouth of a whale. A ribbed curtain, swaying as it gains on them. The town lights have gone, but Ulli still knows where they were. She clings on to knowing where they were as the snow closes in on Edith and Ulli and wipes out the colours of cap and greatcoat, scarf and bold bottle-green tights until it's all one whirlpool of white. Ulli thinks of the current, a long smooth muscle flexing itself under them. Edith's cap has been torn off by the wind, and her wild brown hair flares upward, crusted with snow, snaking and streaming above her head like the locks of a Medusa. Edith's mouth is wide and her teeth are bared and white. Surely, thinks Ulli, she can't be laughing?

Girls on Ice

If you were to take a photograph of Edith and Ulli now, they would be dots. Black and white, merging to grey. Look closely and you won't see their images at all, just two darker splodges on a pale background, like a graze on the paper. They'll look as accidental and as unconvincing as those photographs taken to prove the appearance of ghosts.

Enlarged, Edith and Ulli would be cell-like clumps of dots, like embryos held together in the loose grip of one particular moment before the wind changed, before the snow covered them or stopped falling, before they reached or failed to reach the shore.